How to Photograph a Cowboy...
by Brianne Gainsborough

1. Get permission from his father to follow him around for two weeks. Never ask the cowboy directly—they tend to be loners.

2. Find out what time the cowboy gets up in the morning, then wake up a half an hour earlier. Be ready and waiting with your camera—but tread lightly, even cowboys can roll out of bed on the wrong side.

3. Keep up with the cowboy's every move—and never, ever let him see you sweat. He's just itching for you to throw in the towel and hightail it back to the big city—don't give him the satisfaction.

4. And finally, make sure that you and your brooding cowboy get a chance to spend a night in the wilderness under the star-spangled sky...and don't forget to make a wish!

Dear Reader,

I got a speeding ticket once. Okay, okay, I've gotten speeding tickets twice. Unfortunately, neither ticket turned into a romance with the cop who stopped me. All I ended up with was a court date (much less fun than a dinner date, I promise you) and a fine. Author Patricia Hagan clearly has better things in mind for her characters, though. Pick up *Groom on the Run* and you'll see what I mean. Because when policewoman Liz Casey stops Steve Miller for speeding, all sorts of interesting and exciting things ensue. Like sparks, like romance…and like a very difficult working relationship when she discovers *he's* a cop, too. Pretty soon you can forget misdemeanor speeding and go straight to love in the first degree!

You'll love our second book for the month, too— Marie Ferrarella's *Cowboys Are for Loving*. This is the second in her miniseries THE CUTLERS OF THE SHADY LADY RANCH. Kent Cutler is a cowboy through and through, and he's flat-out not interested in having any city girls hanging around the ranch. Although there's something about Brianne Gainsborough that…well, as you'll see, even the toughest cowboy can be roped and tied when the right woman comes along.

Enjoy them both, and rejoin us next month for two more Yours Truly novels, books where Mr. Right is just around the corner.

Yours,

Leslie J. Wainger
Executive Senior Editor

Please address questions and book requests to:
Silhouette Reader Service
U.S.: 3010 Walden Ave., P.O. Box 1325, Buffalo, NY 14269
Canadian: P.O. Box 609, Fort Erie, Ont. L2A 5X3

MARIE FERRARELLA

Cowboys Are for Loving

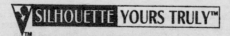

Published by Silhouette Books

America's Publisher of Contemporary Romance

To
John Wayne, Roy Rogers, Ty Hardin and all those
other wonderful cowboy heroes who filled my childhood
with fantastic dreams

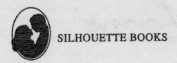 SILHOUETTE BOOKS

ISBN 0-373-52075-1

COWBOYS ARE FOR LOVING

Copyright © 1998 by Marie Rydzynski-Ferrarella

This edition published by arrangement with Harlequin Books S.A.

® and TM are trademarks of Harlequin Books S.A., used under license.
Trademarks indicated with ® are registered in the United States Patent
and Trademark Office, the Canadian Trade Marks Office and in other
countries.

Printed in U.S.A.

Dearest Reader,

I have always loved cowboys. When I was a little girl, the TV was full of them. From John Wayne to Lash LaRue to the Cisco Kid, I loved them all. I learned how to speak English (with a Western twang) by watching early John Wayne Westerns and knew the opening theme song to perhaps a hundred Westerns. (I can still sing the "Zorro" theme song at the drop of a hat—ask my kids.) There was just something so terribly romantic about a strong, silent man who would ride to your rescue. (My husband maintains that any man would be silent in my company, since I talk faster than most people can think, but we won't go there.) Of course, at the end of the show, the hero would ride off alone with the lady standing in the distance, watching him go. In my mind, I'd be right there, riding off into that sunset beside him. I didn't believe in hanging back demurely.

For me, the romance continued even after Westerns and I both grew up. The Westerns got more realistic, grittier, and the cowboys are a shade less heroic and more than a little dirtier, but I still love them.

After reading about Kent Cutler, my hero in *Cowboys Are for Loving,* I hope you will, too.

With all my love,

Marie Ferrarella

Stop on by
The Shady Lady Ranch
in Serendipity, Montana,
home of the Cutler brood—five siblings finding love in the most unexpected places!

Zoe McKay m. Jake Cutler

WILL AND THE HEADSTRONG FEMALE (Yours Truly, 11/98)	Will Cutler m. ?
THE LAW AND GINNY MARLOW (Yours Truly, 1/99)	Quint Cutler m. ?
COWBOYS ARE FOR LOVING (Yours Truly, 9/98)	Kent Cutler m. Brianne Gainsborough
FIONA AND THE SEXY STRANGER (Yours Truly, 7/98)	Hank Cutler m. Fiona Reilly
A MATCH FOR MORGAN (Yours Truly, 3/99)	Morgan Cutler m. ?

1

"No, absolutely not. I am not letting some strange woman into my life." Kent Cutler's voice, usually so low-keyed, was raised, filling every corner of the spacious living room.

Jake Cutler glared at his middle child. With five children, you would have thought that at least one of them wouldn't have been born stubborn to the bone. But even as a child, Kent had had his own mind. At eight, he had already staked his claim by carving his initials on the baseboard by the living-room fireplace and taken the first step toward the rest of his life.

Jake huffed his annoyance. "If you ask me, you could do with a woman in your life, strange or otherwise." Glancing at his wife, Zoe, Jake saw her reproving look, but pretended not to. "Hell, boy, I'm beginning to worry about you and your horse."

The remark didn't bother Kent. His hide had grown thick over the years, by necessity. He'd endured much worse from his siblings and given back as good as he'd gotten. But this was his father, so he shrugged off the dig.

"Well, don't be. The horse is spoken for." His

temper drew a coarse, dark line beneath his easy humor. "And as for me, I should have been spoken *to*, about this crazy idea."

Not, he added silently, that it would have done any good. There was no way in hell he would have ever agreed to let some woman dog his tracks, camera in hand, no matter how diplomatically his father had broached the ridiculous idea.

Because it meant so much to Zoe, Jake attempted to hang on to the frayed ends of his own temper. "You *are* being spoken to about it."

Brows the color of wheat browned by the sun drew together over an almost flawless nose, an unintended gift from his father's side of the family. Kent looked darkly at his father. "One day before she's supposed to arrive is cutting it a little short, don't you think?"

The timing had been intentional, Jake silently admitted. A man knew his own children. Knew, too, all their bad habits. Temper gave way, temporarily, to a smug smile. "Gives you less time to stew about it," Jake told his son.

The expression on Kent's chiseled face was deceptively mild. Both parents recognized the storm brewing beneath.

"I don't have to stew about it. The answer's still no." Kent saw his father open his mouth to retort. He leaned over the shortest of the Cutler men, bringing his face directly before Jake's. "No," Kent repeated with emphasis.

Flaring tempers and dueling temperaments were nothing new to Zoe. She'd put up with displays of both for most of her married life. She'd even entered the fray a time or two herself, although this time all she wanted was to see the flag of truce run up the flagpole.

With a gentling hand on her son's arm, Zoe intervened, hoping to make him come around. "Kent, she's the daughter of an old family friend—"

There was little Kent would deny his mother, but his privacy—his space—was very precious to him. If he were to give it up, it would not be to acquiesce to the whims of some woman he'd never met and, as far as he was concerned, didn't care to meet.

"Fine." With a sweep of his hand, Kent indicated his father. "Let Dad show her around the Shady Lady. He's got the time for it. Me, I'm too busy."

Jake spoke up before Zoe had a chance to. He didn't like being put in a position where he had to go back on a promise. A man's word still counted for something in Jake's world. And Kent, like it or not, belonged to that world.

"She doesn't want to be 'shown around.'" His friend had made that quite clear. "She wants to see what a working ranch is like, firsthand. She wants to take pictures of you sweating."

That was probably how she had put it, too, Kent thought in disgust. "See the cowboy sweat." Typical urban thinking. Ranch life was something that fell under the heading of entertainment to people who drank their water from a fancy bottle instead of from a tap.

Kent leveled a gaze at his father. "Seems to me the girl needs help."

This needed a woman's touch, Zoe thought. Much as she loved Jake, he had a tendency to be heavy-handed, pounding something into the ground with a rock where a light tap would do. She moved in front of Jake, as if to physically block his next words.

"Yes, she does. She needs your help, Kent," Zoe insisted, and made a personal appeal. "Brian Gainsborough used to be the dearest friend your father had in the world. He was best man at our wedding." As naturally as breathing, Zoe slipped her hand into her husband's. "When he called out of the blue, asking if we'd help his daughter and put her up while she's out here in Montana, doing a magazine series on ranching, we saw no harm in saying that we would."

"There isn't any harm in it," Kent agreed amiably. He heard his father sigh with relief. In the next breath, Kent snatched victory back. "But the 'we' includes you and Dad, not me." Putting on his tan, sweat-worn hat, he pulled it low over his eyes. "Now, if you'll excuse me, I've got an appointment with a branding iron, several skittish head of cattle and a couple of new hands who need some training."

With an air of finality, Kent turned and headed for the front door.

It was Jake's turn to raise his voice, calling after his son, "This isn't settled yet."

"Yes," Kent tossed over his shoulder, never breaking stride, "it is."

And, in his innocence, he really thought it was.

This wasn't the first time he'd bucked his father and he didn't intend on being railroaded into agreeing to go along with this.

They were talking about his privacy, something he valued right up there with life, liberty and the pursuit of happiness. Happiness to Kent Cutler meant being left alone to go his own way, do what needed doing. It meant not being interfered with.

But Kent hadn't counted on Brianne Gainsborough. Hadn't counted on the fact that ever since she was a little girl, Brianne always had managed to get what she set out to get once she put her mind to it. Hadn't counted on the fact that Brianne could talk faster than a high-priced auctioneer in a fever pitch. And Kent definitely hadn't counted on the fact that she'd turn out to be the most beautiful woman he had ever seen, on or off the TV, an item he didn't much have time for and even less use for.

No, he hadn't counted on any of that.

Which was why, when Zoe Cutler sent one of the hands to bring her son to the main house, Kent responded in person rather than sending an excuse, mistakenly feeling invulnerable because he was wrapped up in his own confidence.

Slightly put off by having to put in an appearance while in the midst of his day's work, and believing that this was only going to take a few minutes, he arrived at the house without bothering to change or even shake the dust off his clothes.

The first thing he heard when he opened the door

was his father's booming voice. The lady on the receiving end of his oration had her back toward the doorway and Kent. Taking stock of the enemy while still standing safely hidden in the hall, Kent was immediately aware of blond hair, falling straight as a waterfall to the woman's waist.

A highly impractical hairdo, he thought, though he had to admit it was mildly pleasing to the eye.

"You don't look a thing like your old man," Jake was saying to the woman. A chuckle rumbled from deep within his forty-two-inch chest. "Who would have thought that ugly old son of a gun could have sired a filly as beautiful as you?"

Zoe rolled her eyes, shaking her head. After all these years, she was used to Jake's outspokenness, but she knew it could put some people off. "You'll have to forgive Jake, Brianne. He's not accustomed to minding his manners."

Kent heard a laugh in response that sounded like warm honey, thick and rich as it poured over him.

"Forgive him?" Brianne's smile took in her entire countenance, as well as her audience. "I'm flattered. Jake obviously loves horses." When she laid her hand on his arm, Brianne's touch was familiar, as if she'd known Jake Cutler all her life. "That means I've just been paid a very high compliment. And I won't tell Dad what you said if you don't." To seal the bargain, she winked at Jake. "But if you're wondering, I've been told that I look like my mother."

Jake nodded. Brian Gainsborough had a broad, amiable face that brought to mind an overly friendly

Saint Bernard or Newfoundland puppy. "That would explain why you're pretty as a picture. You should be in front of a camera, not behind it."

"Oh, but I love being behind a camera." She looked at the thirty-five millimeter on the coffee table, lying with the rest of her things that had been brought into the house. "I've always had a passion of photography. I've been snapping pictures since I was four years old."

Great, Kent thought. *Just what the doctor ordered, an obsessive woman.*

The look on Zoe's face was apologetic. "I'm afraid that Kent might need a little coaxing. A lot, actually," she amended with a sigh. "This is a busy time of the year at the Shady Lady. There were a lot of calves born this spring—"

Zoe knew she was making excuses, but she was trying to find some way to soften the blow in the event that Kent couldn't be won over. There were times when there was no persuading him, no matter what. If not for Morgan, Zoe would have said that Kent was the most stubborn of her children.

Zoe didn't get far with her apology.

"Wonderful," Brianne enthused. "I'll make the calves the focus of this section of the series."

When she saw the dismayed look on her hostess's face, Brianne hesitated, wondering what she'd said wrong. And then she realized that Zoe wasn't looking at her, but at the doorway behind her.

Turning, Brianne caught her first glimpse of Kent Cutler. She wasn't disappointed.

The man seemed to be wearing half the ranch on his body and his clothes. And it looked damn attractive from where she was standing. What she saw beneath the layers of dirt and dust fit right in with the piece she was writing. Despite his less-than-pristine appearance, Kent cut a very romantic figure. A modern-day cowboy. The man was tall and rangy, with muscles that owed nothing to hours of pumping iron at any classy gym. They had obviously been built up over hours of honest, hard toil. His dark blond hair, long and curling at the ends, contrasted sharply with his deeply bronzed skin.

But Kent Cutler's eyes were his most startling feature. They were so outstandingly blue they demanded immediate attention.

They certainly had hers.

"Kent," Zoe's voice was just a tad reproachful, the way it had sounded to Kent when he'd arrived late and dirty at the dinner table as a boy. "You're dusty."

Kent carelessly shrugged one shoulder, but kept his eyes trained on Brianne as if he expected her to strike suddenly, like a rattler.

"The cattle didn't seem to mind," he finally said evenly.

He entered the room slowly, like a mountain lion testing out terrain that had once been familiar but could prove dangerous nonetheless. He wasn't exactly sure why he'd even bothered to respond to his mother's summons. Probably because he had a soft spot in his heart for her. They clashed, as did he and his father, but at bottom the bond between Kent and his parents was strong. He'd never directly offend either of them by ignoring them, although this was one of those times he surely wished he could.

"Why should they? You blend in perfectly." Brianne snapped the photograph so quickly that it took Kent a second to realize that the flash before his eyes had come from her camera, and not her wide grin.

Instinct had him blocking his face with his hand, but it kicked in too late. The damage had already been done. When he lowered his hand, Brianne made her move and shot another frame.

"Do you have to do that?" He growled the question at her. The woman was faster on the draw than a nineteenth-century gunfighter.

"Yes." Momentarily satisfied, Brianne set the camera back on the table. "It's my job."

He had the feeling she was talking to him the way she would to a slow-witted child. "To be annoying?" he challenged.

Instead of reacting by taking offense, or snapping back at him, as he would have expected any decent person to do, Brianne merely smiled in response. "No, to take photographs. The annoying part depends strictly on my subject."

He didn't care to be smiled at. Not when his temper felt as if it had been rubbed raw. "I'm not your subject, Ms.—"

"Gainsborough," Brianne filled in quickly before either one of his parents could make the unnecessary introduction. If she was any judge of character, the dusty cowboy knew exactly who she was. "No, not entirely," she allowed. "But in part, you are."

He drew himself up, a soldier going one-on-one with the enemy, certain of the victorious outcome. "Oh no, I'm not."

Zoe wet her lips. It seemed the older her son got, the more introverted and unreachable he became. It was all the fault of Brick Taylor's daughter. Rosemary Taylor had turned her son against the whole sex. If it had been up to her, Zoe would have wrung the young girl's neck before she'd have let her hurt Kent. He had never talked about it, but she knew all about the proposal and the flippant refusal that had met it.

Still, that was no excuse for his rudeness now. "Kent can be a little difficult at times." Zoe slanted a look toward her son. It was, she knew, a vast understatement.

Jake saw the tiny lines of distress furrow between his wife's eyebrows. He slipped a supportive arm around Zoe's shoulders.

"All her fault," he told Brianne, but there was affection in his voice. Anyone who knew them knew Jake Cutler worshipped the ground his wife walked on. "Spare the rod, spoil the child."

Zoe raised her chin. "Like you ever raised a hand to any of them."

"Couldn't." He pretended to shrug helplessly. "They were all too fast, and besides, I was afraid of you."

Love, never far away, came into Zoe's dark blue eyes. "And well you should be, Jake Cutler."

Zoe blinked, stifling a small gasp of surprise as the flash on Brianne's camera went off again. Zoe looked at her, confused.

If this shot wasn't a keeper, she wasn't worth her weight in negatives, Brianne thought. "Sorry if I startled you," she said to Zoe. "I just couldn't resist. You make a very nice couple. And this is a story on the whole ranch, not just Kent. My father's told me so much about the Shady Lady Ranch, I just had to see it for myself."

"Hold it. None of it is going to be Kent," Kent corrected Brianne tersely.

What did it take for this woman to get that through her thick head? He was speaking plain enough for an idiot to understand. Just what was her problem?

Brianne swung around to look at him. He hadn't noticed before how large her eyes were. Large and luminous. And maybe a little hypnotic. They seemed to gleam like two blue topaz stones, bombarded by the sun.

They could be beacons, for all he cared, he told himself. A big-eyed look didn't mean anything. It certainly didn't mean she was going to get her way. He had a hell of a lot more important things to do than play wet nurse to some roaming photographer, even if she did come packaged in a neat, tempting bundle.

Outgoing and friendly, Brianne still enjoyed a

good war of wills when the occasion arose. "But you are part of the ranch," she pointed out.

"A very big part," Jake put in. There was pride in every word. They might be stubborn to a fault, but not one of his kids had ever disappointed him when it really mattered. "Kent's been running the ranch for us for the last three years, right after I had that bout of indigestion."

Zoe's eyes narrowed accusingly. "It was a heart attack," she pronounced firmly, looking at Brianne. "Man didn't know the meaning of the words 'slow down.' Always had to be on the go, always knew best."

She loved him, warts and all, but Jake could be absolutely infuriating when he wanted to be. The thought of facing life without him had brought a positive chill to her heart, so Zoe had enlisted all her children's help in convincing Jake that it was time to hand over the reins to Kent. She meant to keep the father of her children around for a good long time.

Jake grinned. He winked broadly at Brianne. "When we all know that it's Zoe who knows best."

They were so cute, Brianne thought. It warmed her to be in the midst of such blatant love.

A tiny sliver of envy pricked her. Kent Cutler and his siblings were lucky people, to have grown up to see this kind of affection expressed in their everyday lives. She loved her father dearly and he was a wonderful man, but for the most part, he'd been absent from her life. Always somewhere else, always busy building up the business that now bore his name.

For Brianne it had been a lonely childhood. Her mother had died when she was very young, so Brianne had enjoyed the company of some very highly paid, very intelligent, kindly nannies. Their kindness notwithstanding, it definitely wasn't the same thing that the Cutler crew had enjoyed.

Too bad all that affection hadn't rubbed off Kent's rough edges, she mused. But that just made the challenge more interesting, and she'd never met a man she couldn't talk her way around, one way or another.

"Yes," Zoe was saying to her. "I do know best. Which is why Kent's handling things around here. Jake and I are rather like the queen of England. Figureheads," she explained after a beat when Jake just looked at her.

"You can be queen of England," Jake told his wife with a snort, then jerked a thumb at himself. "Me, I'm the king."

"There is no king of England," Zoe told him smugly. "Just a prince." The answer gave Jake pause.

Kent shifted. He'd wasted enough time. There was only so much daylight available and he meant to make the most of it. He inclined his head toward his parents, like a vassal giving them their due.

"If your royal highnesses don't mind, I'm going back to my place to get a couple of things and then get back to work."

"You don't live here?" Brianne looked around the large, sprawling ranch house. At first glance, there seemed to be enough room to house the entire clan and then some.

Kent didn't even bother looking over his shoulder. His goal was the door and he meant to reach it. Quickly. "No, I don't."

He would have left the explanation—and the lady—hanging right there. But his mother added, "He lives in a house just a mile and a half from here. Our son Will designed it. He's the architect. You'll be staying here with Jake and me, of course, but maybe you'd like to see Kent's place."

That stopped him in his tracks. He turned slowly around. Just what had gotten into his mother? She usually left him to his own devices. This was a hell of a time to start meddling in his life.

"No, she wouldn't," Kent announced.

And that, he figured, walking out, was that.

Except that it wasn't.

By the time Kent had crossed the threshold and was outside the house, Brianne and the infernal camera that swung like some kind of grotesque appendage at her side had already caught up to him.

"Yes, 'she' would," she contradicted cheerfully. "It's part of your life, isn't it?"

He glared at her. "So's washing. You going to watch me take a shower, too?"

Her grin broadened. "The piece isn't going to be that in-depth."

Although sales, Brianne was certain, would go

through the roof if there were a photo of Kent in the altogether included in the article. There was no doubt in her mind that the body beneath the worn jeans and dirty workshirt was lean and hard. The kind of stuff that fantasies were made of.

She had tenacity, he'd give her that. But he had more, Kent thought, looking down into her determined eyes. She wore an amused expression, he noticed. Just what was there that struck her so funny?

Was she amusing herself, the sophisticated city girl, checking out the country bumpkins?

"The piece isn't going to be at all," he informed Brianne.

Oh yes, it is. I've faced down more stubborn men than you, Kent Cutler, Brianne thought.

"You can't be that camera-shy," she insisted incredulously.

She sounded as if she knew the workings of his mind better than he did. Kent had had just about his fill. "Being camera-shy has nothing to do with it—"

"Then you think I'll get in the way." She didn't give him time to piece together his thoughts, or his rebuttal. "I won't, I promise. You won't even know I'm there."

Almost involuntarily, his eyes swept over her. Brianne Gainsborough smelled like lilacs and looked like blond sin on toast. Even blindfolded and hog-tied, there was no way he wouldn't know she was there.

His eyes darkened ominously. "What part of 'no' don't you understand?"

She threw him by laughing and saying, "All of it." And then she made matters more difficult by smiling up at him as if they were the best of friends, instead of on opposite sides of a very private fence. "Be a sport, Kent. Two weeks, that's all I ask." She held up two fingers. "Two weeks out of your life. I'll be gone before you know it." Her smiled deepened a little, just enough to give it breadth and substance. "This series is very important to me."

It was, he realized. He could see it in those damn blue eyes of hers. His own narrowed. The struggle with his better instincts told him he was about to make a very large mistake. He tried to compensate. "What's in it for me if I say yes?"

The smile widened. She could smell capitulation. Brianne was a magnanimous victor. "What do you want there to be in it for you?"

Kent had no answer, because he hadn't expected the question. Foolishly, he thought his own would make the woman back off.

"I'll let you know," was all he muttered.

Yes!

Triumphant, Brianne surprised him for the second time in ten minutes. This time the instrument of surprise wasn't a camera. It was formed by two arms and two lips as Brianne threw the former around his neck and pressed the latter against his mouth. Quickly, fleetingly and completely on impulse.

Just the way a mule kicked.

2

He resisted only because it took him completely by surprise. A sudden movement Kent hadn't, not in his wildest dreams, anticipated. Strangers didn't kiss you, certainly not with such gusto and feeling. They shook your hand. Maybe.

This was no handshake.

The next moment, sensations burrowed in, muting Kent's surprise. Dissolving it. Delicious sensations that he hadn't been prepared to sample.

But wasn't unprepared to enjoy.

Instincts rather than thought had him bringing his arms around to encircle her and something far more basic than thought caused him to lightly glide his hands along the curve of her back.

She tasted like sugar-dusted strawberries picked right in the heart of summer, and her kiss made his head spin like he'd just downed a shot of hundred-year-old bourbon—precisely three fingers' worth, rapidly, on an empty stomach.

He'd never come up against anyone like her.

Without realizing just what he was doing, Kent pulled her closer, trying to get to the heart of this dizzying feeling. To have more before there wasn't any left.

Or until he returned to his senses, whichever happened first.

But even as the sensations crowded around him, blotting out everything else, he could feel her drawing away. Could feel her lips leaving his.

Sanity returned, chasing away the golden hues that had so quickly set up housekeeping within him. He tried not to look as thoroughly rattled as he felt.

Well, that had certainly been more than she'd bargained for, Brianne thought. Her body felt hot, flushed. She ran her hand along the back of her neck, certain that there were singe marks all along it as well as the rest of her body. What had begun in a burst of enthusiasm had gone on to be quite something else. Something disturbingly more.

The "burst" had roused a sleeping volcano. She could feel, even now, the rumblings vibrating within her. She actually felt a little shaky, as if some of the bones in her knees had been subjected to meltdown. And if it wouldn't have been so damn obvious, she would have run her tongue along her lips, just to savor his taste.

He had definitely aroused her. She wondered if he'd done it intentionally, then decided by the look on Kent's face that he hadn't. He looked as stunned as she felt. That was comforting, and yet exciting to her at the same time.

Grinning, Brianne took a step away from him.

With a huge sigh, she pretended to fan herself with her hand. "No wonder ladies love cowboys."

Kent had never been known to be overly talkative, but it wasn't usually because someone had robbed him of the ability to speak. The way Brianne had done just now. It took him a minute to even find his tongue, another to get it in working order again.

Trying to collect himself, to gather wits that seemed to have spilled out like so many peas rolling away from an upended can, he stood staring at Brianne. At the tight, firm body encased in worn jeans and a denim jacket, both of which adhered to her every curve as if they comprised a comfortable, second skin.

He hadn't a clue what to make of her.

Kent wasn't altogether sure that anyone *could* make Brianne Gainsborough out. At least, not unless they had an advanced degree in some sort of pretentious-sounding course of study.

The pit of his stomach felt like warm jelly. Just what the hell had happened here?

He tried to scowl, but he couldn't quite get his face to work that way. The best he could manage was to look solemn.

"You kiss everyone like that?"

Brianne's pulse had finally stopped racing faster than the speed of light. It was a start.

She took another long breath before answering. "Nope. Only when I'm happy." Her eyes smiled at him just as warmly as her lips did. Maybe even more so. "And you, Kent Cutler, have made me very happy."

Well, it wasn't mutual. He didn't like feeling as if he'd just been dropped headfirst into a whirlpool, and he wasn't about to stand around, waiting for a repeat performance. Nor did he intend to help perpetuate that look on her face, no matter how well the woman could press two lips together—and who taught her to kiss like that, anyway?

No, it didn't matter, he told himself almost immediately. He didn't care who'd taught her. All he cared about was finding a way to make her leave. So if Brianne Gainsborough's happiness depended on dogging his every move, she was going to find herself unhappy very soon.

Without commenting on the sentiment she'd just expressed, Kent strode over to the horse he'd left hitched to one of the porch columns and swung into his saddle. Just as he made contact with the well-oiled leather, he heard the annoying sound of her camera greedily stealing a little more of his privacy.

This time, he did scowl. And growl. "Do you have to start that already?"

Brianne slid the protective casing around the camera again. The action was so much a part of her, she wasn't even aware of doing it.

"I don't believe in wasting time or opportunities." She slung the camera over her shoulder like a handbag, then lifted one hand up to him. "Give me a hand up?"

Now what was she up to? "Up to what?"

She would have thought that was rather obvious. Determined to remain polite, she nodded at his mount. "Your horse. I can't get on behind you unless you give me your hand."

And he wasn't about to, either, Kent thought. He had no desire to go galloping off into the sunset with her. He felt sure that was what was on her mind. Some fool romantic notion like that. He and his way of life probably represented nothing more than a caricature to her, a twisted version of what really existed.

Instead, looking at her darkly, he gestured to her parked car. "Something's wrong with your car?"

She didn't bother looking over her shoulder at the rented vehicle. "Nothing." She patted the quarter horse's powerful neck, genuine appreciation in her eyes. "I just want to get into the proper mood, that's all."

Proper mood for what? he wondered warily.

He noted the look in her eyes. Well, at least the woman knew good horseflesh when she saw it. But that didn't change the fact that he'd only known her fifteen minutes and she was already getting to be one royal pain in the butt.

With a disgusted expression he didn't bother to disguise, Kent took her hand and jerked Brianne up behind him.

He'd give her the proper mood, all right. Just wait until tomorrow, he silently promised himself. When he was finished showing this woman with the pricey boots the way a real working ranch operated, she'd be content to do the rest of her research watching old Westerns on one of the cable stations that his sister, Morgan, was always telling him about.

If he was rougher with her than she'd expected, Brianne gave no indication. No squeals of protest or distress escaped her lips as she hit the saddle. Instead, she laced her arms tightly around his waist and announced, "Okay, I'm ready."

She might be ready, Kent thought darkly, but he wasn't.

He wasn't ready for the odd flicker of warmth that wafted through him when she laid her cheek against his shoulder. Wasn't ready for the way his body reacted when she pressed hers against him as he took off. Nope, he just wasn't ready.

Annoyed with himself as well as with her, Kent purposely urged his horse into a full gallop.

Instead of uttering a plea to slow down, Gainsborough deliberately rankled him by holding on tighter, and then had the audacity to laugh as if he'd just taken her for a ride at an amusement park.

Things went from bad to impossible during the short trip from his parents' house to his. Impossible for him. Kent didn't appreciate the fact that her laughter got under his skin, or that the tips of her hair whip around so that they teased his face, making something in his belly tighten.

And he sure as hell didn't care for the fact that he could still taste her mouth on his and that it created a sudden yen within him for sugar-dusted strawberries.

A man with a ranch to oversee just didn't have time for this kind of nonsense. Dalliances and distractions were all well and good for Hank, or Will or even Quint. His brothers could let their minds wander for a bit without incurring any inconvenient consequences. But if he let his wander, it would throw his timing off. You couldn't rope a calf if your timing was off. And branding became a real problem if you weren't focused on it. No, he didn't have time for this.

Annoyance at the way his own body seemed to be mutinying against him heightened. Kent reined in his horse, purposely coming to an abrupt halt in front of the small single-story ranch house that Will had put so much effort into designing.

Will had tried to create a place that would be a comfortable home for his brother and yet reflect the essence that made him Kent. So the house and the furnishings within were utilitarian without being sparse, strong without being overpowering.

His house.

Kent looked at it as if seeing it for the first time. Trying to see it through a stranger's eyes. The structure stood proud and alone against the afternoon sun. The house suited him, he thought. Once he'd fancied sharing this place with a certain someone who might have added a few light touches to it, but now that notion was gone.

Just as well. He liked things the way they were. There was no reason for change.

"We're here," he announced, swinging one leg in front of him over the saddle horn.

Without a backward glance to see if she was secure, Kent slid off and hit the ground. He left Brianne entirely without support, expecting her to tumble awkwardly off the horse. He wasn't about to let her hurt herself. He just figured he'd catch her on the way down. The jostling might do her some good. Might even get her brain functioning better than it was now so that she'd give this up, or at least find someone else to hound.

But he was doomed to be disappointed on a lot of scores today. Brianne dismounted the horse as fluidly as if she'd been riding all of her life. As if Amber Whiskey was her horse instead of his.

Because he was going to ride out again soon, he didn't lead the horse to the stable. Instead, he secured one rein around a post to keep Whiskey from wandering off.

His attention wasn't on the horse. It was on the annoying woman he was being saddled with. "Where did you learn to ride?"

"New York." Brianne laughed when she saw the dubious look on his face. "They have horses in New York."

"Central Park." He said it contemptuously, as if there was a caste system involving horses and the ones in the city were the lowest of the low.

"And upstate," Brianne pointed out. His view of the East seemed to be as narrow as some people's view of the West. Maybe the people who were going to read her article weren't the only ones in for a learning experience, she mused.

"You don't sound like you're from New York." His tone was almost accusing, as if she'd somehow tried to trick him.

Brianne ran her hand over Whiskey's muzzle. The horse whinnied, but kept still. "I'm not."

"But you just said—"

Since she was going to be intruding into his life, she thought it only fair that he know a few things about hers. Unlike Kent, she wasn't particularly jealous of her privacy. On the contrary, her life was an open book.

"That's where I learned how to ride, not where I lived. At least, not for long," she amended. "We traveled around a lot when I was younger." "We" meant herself, her father and whatever nanny happened to be with them at the time. Because of the frequent moves, she'd had more than her share. "My father went wherever the money was."

If she thought he was going to get suckered in by this poor-little-rich-girl scenario, she was about to be disappointed. Whatever she had or had not endured in her past meant nothing to him. And he wasn't about to begin trading information, if that's what she was after.

Still, she had made him just the slightest bit curious. He couldn't see his father and hers as best friends. They sounded as if they came from two different worlds. "Just what is it that your father does?"

In the beginning, it had been anything, in order to get by. Brian Gainsborough had seen no shame in trying his hand at a great many ventures, just to see what would take off for him. He'd finally found what turned out to be his true calling when Brianne was ten years old.

"I guess the best way to sum it up is to say that he's an entrepreneur." And what went into that would take a whole afternoon to explain. For both their sakes, she decided to skip it. "But I'm not here to do a piece on my father. I'm here to do one on you—that is, on the ranch," she added quickly before his face darkened completely. Patting the horse affectionately on the rump, Brianne took her camera out of its case and stepped up to Kent's front door. She offered him her best smile. "Show me your place?"

He placed his hand over the lens of the camera, which was dangling from the strap at her shoulder. His eyes met hers. His were somber. "As long as you don't take any pictures of it."

He had to be kidding. That was the whole point of seeing the house. "But—"

Kent didn't waver. "This part isn't negotiable. You can take all the photographs you want of my parents' house. They seem to like the idea." Though how, he didn't understand. "And the ranch belongs to all of us, so I can't very well stop you there, either." He jerked a thumb behind him at the door. "But this is mine. You can come in, you can look around." He probably couldn't stop her, anyway.

"But no pictures, understood?" He looked intently into her eyes. "Do we have a deal?"

"I—"

He could see the protest, the makings of a debate there in her eyes. Eyes that could make a man sweat if he let his imagination go to places it had no business going.

"Do we have a deal?" he repeated.

Brianne sighed reluctantly. If there was no other way. "We have a deal."

She knew she had no choice at the moment. Maybe, if things went smoothly, she could talk him out of his stand later. If not, well, she supposed she could live with this bargain. She could understand the need to keep a part of yourself tucked away. Everyone needed a tiny space to retreat to, a piece of your soul that was yours alone. Kent's was just larger than most.

His hand remained on the lens. He looked as if he didn't believe her, she thought.

He didn't. If she was supposedly giving him her word, he wanted backup. Proof. He pointed to the case. "Put the lens cap on."

Brianne wasn't accustomed to being distrusted. "What?"

He was hot, sweaty and at the end of his temper. "You heard me, put the damn cap on."

For a tiny fraction of a second, she toyed with the temptation of telling him what he could do with his order. But the feeling passed quickly. It was compromise that won ground, not opposition. Still smiling amiably, she took out the cap and moving his hand out of the way, snapped it over the lens.

"Not very trusting, are you?"

Kent didn't care for the amusement in her eyes. Like she was laughing at him. He watched her tuck the camera back into its case.

"That all depends on who or what we're talking about. I trust my horse. I trust my family, my friends—" his tone dropped as his eyes unintentionally flickered over her mouth "—my instincts."

She cocked her head to one side, studying him. "And what do your instincts tell you?"

That was easy. There was no mystery about that. "That you're trouble and to run like hell."

She just looked back at him as if she knew all about him. "But you're not going to."

"I don't run." He shrugged, then deliberately kept his eyes on hers. "And it seems to mean a lot to my parents to have me be nice to you. Unfortunately, part of that means letting you tag along." He blew out a large breath. "So all right, you can tag along." The warning was in his expression before it was ever on his lips. "But the first minute you get in the way—"

"I'm history." It wasn't a guess. She knew. At the first infraction that rubbed him the wrong way, he'd dump her like so much unwanted, dirty laundry.

Despite himself, he couldn't repress the hint of a smile that flirted with his mouth. "As long as we understand each other."

She had her doubts about that being strictly true.

It was all one-sided. "In order for that to happen, I think you need to understand me—"

Kent had no interest in hearing anything she might feel necessary to offer in the way of explanations. He already knew more about her than he needed to. "Oh, I understand you all right, lady."

She arched an eyebrow. "Oh, really?" A bemused smile playing on her lips, Brianne crossed her arms before her. "And what, exactly, is it that you understand?"

Since she asked, he pulled no punches. "That you're here to do some kind of a fluff piece to entertain bored, urban cowboy wanna-bes. Or maybe to feed the daydreams for some equally bored bunch of women who think that there's something romantic about the kind of life we lead out here." He had no patience with either group.

Just what had happened to him to make him view life in such somber hues? Brianne refused to believe that he'd always been this way. People weren't born with this black outlook—something made them that way. From what she could see, his parents were terrific, so the reason had to be elsewhere. A woman? She rolled the idea over in her mind.

"Romantic," she contradicted, "can be anywhere." She saw the contempt in his eyes, but she pushed on. "Romantic depends on the person, not the circumstances." She believed that from the bottom of her heart. "A one-room shack can be a romantic setting. A palace can be a cold prison. It's who you're with that counts, not where."

He wasn't impressed, she could see that. Well, that was his privilege, but she wanted no mistakes made about her work. She took that very seriously.

"And for your information, I'm not here to do a 'fluff piece' as you call it. If that were my intent, I could have just as easily accomplished it by working out of my office and using my imagination." Looking up, she leaned toward him. "I've got a very healthy imagination," she said significantly, "but I'm here for the truth. The dirt and the grit and the work," she added, when he said nothing.

Kent snorted as he opened his front door. "You'll have your share of all three if you follow me around."

She smiled serenely as she stepped over the threshold. "I'm counting on it."

He sincerely doubted it.

Morning always seemed to come too early. Kent squeezed his eyes shut, as if that could make the hands on the clock move backward, giving him back a little more time. It didn't. Kent sighed.

He was a morning person because he had to be, not because he liked it. What he most wanted at this moment was to cling to his mattress and sleep until the sun was more than just a hint on the horizon. But he knew better than that.

With another sigh, he threw back the thin covers. There was still a lot of branding to do and fences to see to, not to mention the acquisition of a new Black

Angus bull to negotiate. None of that was about to do itself.

Still more than half-asleep, Kent slowly dragged himself up against the headboard until he was in a sitting position. That accomplished, he next set about gathering enough energy to swing his legs over the edge and have his feet make contact with the floor. It took him several minutes.

From there, he stumbled off in the general direction of the bathroom. Though right about now it seemed rather barbaric, he knew that the only thing that was guaranteed to bring him back from the realm of the undead was a shower. A cold one.

In the stall, he gritted his teeth and turned on the faucet. Gooseflesh threatened to overpower his taut muscles as it sprang up all over his body in response to the steely needles of cold water that were assaulting him.

"God, there's got to be a better way than this," he muttered under his breath.

Braced, eyes finally opened, Kent quickly scrubbed the residue of sleep away. Less than five minutes later he was out, his towel precariously anchored at his waist, watery footprints marking his path, wet hair plastered against his neck. Now that he was awake enough to form coherent thoughts, he remembered why he'd dreaded this particular morning so much.

She was going to be coming along.

Not for long, he'd lay odds. Not after Gainsborough saw just what he meant by getting an early start. Early to her probably meant nine o'clock.

Kent smiled to himself, combing his wet hair out of his eyes with his fingers. Just as soon as he got some coffee into him, he'd ride over to his parents' house. He was looking forward to waking her up and—

Kent stopped and sniffed the air.

Was that—?

Coffee, he definitely smelled coffee. But that was impossible. The automatic coffeemaker Morgan had given him had died an unnatural death a couple of weeks ago, unable to handle the thick brew he liked to drink. He hadn't found time to go into town to get himself a new one. Coffee, for the last two weeks, had been coming from an old battered drip pot that took forever.

Kent dismissed the aroma. Had to be his imagination working overtime.

But his imagination had never been that good. He could swear he smelled coffee. Strong, rich coffee.

Curious now, Kent headed toward the kitchen. Maybe Quint had dropped by. The sheriff of Serendipity thought nothing of letting himself into his brother's house. Of course, it might help if he remembered to lock his doors. But out here, nobody really did. Especially not when they were so far away from everything.

Kent took three steps into the kitchen, then stopped dead. The woman he was looking forward

to dragging from her warm bed was standing in his
kitchen, doing something at his stove.

Brianne turned around at the sound of wet feet
padding along a scuffed wooden floor. She smiled
brightly at him, acting as if her being here was the
most natural thing in the world.

"Morning. You didn't answer when I knocked."
Her eyes skimmed over his wet torso. So that was
what they meant by a washboard stomach. The towel
looked in jeopardy of coming undone at his very next
move. Her smile widened. "Nice outfit."

3

With a start, Kent clamped his hand on the knot that was slipping, inching its way farther down his hipbone.

He glared accusingly at Brianne. "What are you doing here?"

She looked at him, her smile as bright as a newly minted silver dollar, as innocent as fresh snow. "Making coffee."

Kent gritted his teeth together. "I mean, *what are you doing here?*"

Was she too obtuse to get his meaning? She had no business being in his house like this. Why wasn't she where she was supposed to be? In bed, asleep so that he could wake her up.

Maybe this wasn't a good time to tease him, Brianne decided. She had come armed with all the provisions that went into making a hearty breakfast, courtesy of his parents. Jake had figured it was the best way to arrange a truce between her and his son and had said so. Brianne had no problem with making a meal or two if it meant that things could go more smoothly between them. She believed in doing whatever worked.

Wrapping a pot holder that had definitely seen better days around the handle, she eased the coffeepot off the stove.

"Your mother said I should come in if you didn't answer the door on the third knock. She told me that sometimes you were very hard to rouse in the morning as a boy. Your father said strong coffee usually did the trick, so I made coffee." Jake's exact advice was to pour it on Kent if all else failed, but she didn't think Kent wanted to hear that. Holding up the pot, she looked at him brightly. "Want some?"

Yes, he wanted coffee. Badly. But there was something he wanted even more. Where the hell did she get the gall to come barging in like this? And why had his parents suddenly ganged up against him? "What I want is privacy."

"I didn't come into your shower, did I?" Her eyes sparkled with laughter that made him want to wrap his hands around her very pretty throat and squeeze.

He could see her doing it, too. Walking right into his shower stall as if she had every right in the world to invade it. "I guess I should be grateful for small favors."

Brianne was busy opening cupboards. She found what she was looking for on her second try and took out a mug. He looked like the mug type, she thought. No fancy little cups for Kent Cutler, just something sturdy he could wrap his hands around.

Her eyes touched his face fleetingly. "Now you're

catching on." Filling the mug to the rim, she moved it across the counter toward him. "Coffee's hot. Thick and black, the way you like it," she added when he made no move to take it.

It was a short battle. The need for caffeine got the better of him. Kent picked the mug up in both hands and took a long, hearty gulp. He nearly scalded his tongue, but it was worth it. Every nerve ending had snapped to attention.

Revived, he studied her suspiciously over the rim. "How would you know how I like it?"

"I asked," she answered simply.

She'd asked a lot of questions about him last night over supper with his parents and one of his brothers. Between Zoe, Jake and Will, an interesting picture of Kent Cutler was beginning to emerge. Whether he realized it or not, that picture fit right into the stereotypical image that some people had of the vanishing cowboy.

Why not? she mused. Stereotypes were all based on something.

Pausing to take a sip from her own mug, Brianne couldn't help noticing that coverage was receding from his hipline again. Kent was going to have to move fast if he wanted to maintain his modesty.

She raised her eyes demurely, catching her tongue between her teeth. "I think your towel is heading due south."

Kent made a grab for it, but not quite soon enough. It was at his knee before he knew it. Swearing, he jerked it back into place. Annoyed, embarrassed, he half expected to see a flash and hear the grating sound of Brianne's camera as it commemorated the moment, despite their agreement.

But when he looked, her hands were empty.

It wasn't hard to guess what he was thinking. On some levels, Kent Cutler was not as complicated a man as he undoubtedly believed himself to be. She tried very hard not to grin.

"Don't worry, I'm not into that kind of photograph." She glanced at her watch, wrestling silently with her conscience as she tried not to let her line of vision drift his way again until his dignity was restored. The word magnificent, she decided, had been created with Kent Cutler in mind—in every sense.

She nodded toward the front of the house and what lay beyond. "I thought you said you wanted to get an early start."

The only way Kent could be sure that the incident wouldn't repeat itself was to keep one hand on his towel at all times. He grasped the mug with the other. Before he could drain the contents, she was filling it again.

"At what, strangling you?" he growled.

"At doing whatever it is you planned to do today." She moved back toward the stove.

For the first time, he saw that there was a large frying pan on one of the burners. Kent became aware of other aromas mingling with the scent of coffee. Aromas that teased his senses, whetted his appetite. Some he could place and connect directly to what she was doing at the stove.

But one scent in particular, the one that clung to her, rose above the others, eluded definition.

Maybe it was best that way.

"Why don't you get dressed?" she suggested pleasantly, flipping a golden pancake over on the pan. "I'll stay here and make you breakfast."

He wanted no part of any meal she made. It probably tasted like stale, burnt cardboard anyway. A woman who looked like that couldn't possibly cook, too. Besides, if he caught his father's drift, she was well-off. She probably had a housekeeper.

"I'll get dressed *and* make my own breakfast," he shot back at her over his shoulder.

He heard her laugh to herself and murmur, "And they say women are stubborn."

Kent began to calculate just what two weeks boiled down to in actual minutes. There were a hell of a lot of them.

He could maintain silence like no one Brianne had ever met. She'd served him a plateful of pancakes, with bacon and toast on the side. He'd almost consumed it all and still hadn't said a word.

She stood it for as long as she could, then asked, "Well?"

Kent shrugged carelessly, popping the last bit of toast into his mouth. He waited until he swallowed before answering. "Not bad."

Actually, it was the best breakfast he'd had in a very long time, but he saw no reason to tell her that. He'd be damned if he'd let her think she was getting on his good side. Because she wasn't. Not with a meal or a cup of coffee, even a damn fine cup of coffee. He couldn't be swayed that easily.

All things considered, Brianne supposed she was lucky to have gotten that much out of him. "I guess, coming from you, that's high praise." She leaned her chin against her upturned hand and studied him. "You don't talk much, do you?"

He slanted a glance in her direction before lowering his eyes to his almost empty plate. "Not unless there's something to say."

And that was where they differed the most. She loved communicating, exchanging ideas, views. Or just sharing a joke. To be closemouthed like this was completely alien to her.

"But there's always something to say, something to comment on," she insisted.

How could he look around him and remain silent? How could he look at a sunset, or a sunrise or a horizon and not be moved to say something to acknowledge it and the way it affected him? She'd kissed him. He wasn't made out of stone. Why did he try to act like it?

She would say that, Kent thought. The woman had probably popped out of her mother's womb talking. "I like silence," he said firmly.

The last thing Brianne wanted to do was to argue with him, especially so early in their relationship. "In its place," she allowed slowly.

"Its place is out here."

Which was why he didn't want her around. She'd

ruin it. He liked the solitude that he felt out here. A
solitude linked with an unspoken camaraderie with
his men as they worked the ranch. With that constantly moving mouth of hers, and that invasive camera, she'd jeopardize all that, never mind that it was
for a limited time. Time was irreplaceable; he didn't
want to lose a single day of it.

Brianne took out a pad and pen and began writing.
Kent stopped, his fork suspended in midair as he
scowled. "What are you doing?"

She glanced up for a moment, then continued making notes before she forgot something. "Writing
down what you just said, about this being the place
for silence."

It wasn't that remarkable. Why did she feel com-
pelled to make something of it? He put his hand in
the way, blocking the page.

"Why?"

The man was more suspicious than a debriefed
spy, Brianne thought. "Because it belongs in the article," she explained patiently. Moving his hand
aside, she wrote as she spoke, her mind shifting between two different planes. "Because I'm trying to
help readers picture the type of man who gravitates
to this kind of life." Finished, she flipped the pad
closed. "Because I can give them a sense of being
out here."

"While sitting in their comfortable chairs, right?"
He had nothing but contempt for men who spent the
better part of their lives with their butts planted on a
soft cushion, being swallowed up by their couches.

Brianne smiled knowingly at him. She was beginning to get his number. "Would you rather that they all came out here to experience it firsthand?"

The very thought of people crowding in on this beautiful land he held so dear could make him break out in a cold sweat.

"Your way's better," he admitted grudgingly.

She didn't bother hiding the triumphant expression that came over her face. "I kind of thought you'd come around."

The moment he laid his fork down, she whisked his plate away to the sink and began washing it.

He didn't like being waited on. It was bad enough he'd let her make breakfast. *Let* wasn't exactly the word. He'd had no choice. The meal had been on the table when he'd returned from the bedroom.

He waved her away from the sink. "No need to do that. Just leave it."

Brianne had no intentions of leaving anything in the sink. The pot and pans she'd used were all washed and dripping dry on the rack and she'd painstakingly cleaned out the coffeepot. She wasn't about to leave a plate dirty.

"I've got nothing else to do." She looked at him over her shoulder. "You're still drinking coffee and I can't take any photographs, remember?"

The fact that she intended to honor their agreement surprised Kent. He'd really thought that he was going to have to get tough with her for that to be enforced. "You're sticking to the deal?"

She looked at him in surprise, as if she couldn't

fathom why he'd doubt her. "Of course. My word's my bond," she told him cheerfully.

Like he believed that, Kent thought.

Brianne looked around. Not finding the towel she was looking for, she dried her hands by wiping them along the seat of her jeans.

Kent felt a sudden, compelling urge to trace the path she'd just forged with his own hands.

With a self-deprecating huff, he blocked the thought. She grinned at him as if she could read his mind.

Probably could, being part witch. Why else had he found himself agreeing to this fool notion that had been forced on him when he could just as easily have said no? More easily, actually.

Probably more than part witch, he amended silently.

Turning the chair around to face her, Brianne straddled it as she sat down opposite him at the table. "So, when do we get started?"

He might as well get this over with. If his plan worked, with luck this would be the last morning he'd have to put up with her.

Kent drained his mug, then rose, leaving it where it was. "Now."

"Great."

With a deft move, Brianne had the mug in the sink, rinsed and draining before Kent reached the threshold. In the next beat, she was right beside him, hat and camera in hand, walking out the door.

He'd already told her once not to bother. It seemed

to him she took pleasure in ignoring whatever she didn't feel like hearing. "Do you always move this fast?"

Brianne's shoulder brushed against his arm as she moved ahead. Turning, she smiled up at Kent, amusement in her eyes.

"Almost." She paused, then added more softly, "Some things, though, I do slowly."

It was on the tip of his tongue to ask what, but he had a sneaking suspicion that he would do well not to hear her answer. It might turn out to be more than he could deal with.

Instead, he slammed the door behind him and headed toward the stable.

His stride was long. Brianne had to hurry to keep up. She knew better than to ask him to slow down.

"I picked out a horse for you," he told her as he walked into the stable.

She wondered if she should be wary or not. "Do you still do your ranching on horseback?"

The last ranch she'd spent time on, the owner conducted all his business from the driver's side of a Jeep, but she had to admit that she couldn't quite picture Kent behind the wheel of an all-terrain vehicle. Never mind that it marred the romance of the setting, Kent was the kind of man who belonged on a horse, not behind an engine.

"Most of it." He resisted most forms of technology. That was for the others, not him. He was a man with few wants, few needs. Simplicity had always been the key to his character. A horse was a great deal simpler than a car. More economical, too. "Some of the others prefer riding around in a Jeep or in a truck. Using a horse gives me a better feel for what I'm doing."

He stopped abruptly when he realized that he'd said more than he meant to. Damn, but she had a way of drawing words out. He was going to have to watch that.

Kent headed for the far stall, berating himself for running off at the mouth. When he turned around, he saw that she was writing in her notepad again. He might have known.

"If you stop to scribble down everything I say, you're going to be left behind," he warned. "I'm not waiting for you."

Brianne already knew that. Making a last hasty note to herself, she capped the pen and tucked the small, lined pad into her purse as she hurried to join him.

"You made that perfectly clear yesterday." Without any awareness of just how sexy she looked doing it, she tossed her hair over her shoulder. "I just wanted to get things down while they were fresh."

Drawing his eyes away from her, Kent merely grunted in response. He picked up a bridle before approaching the horse.

"Do you know how to saddle a horse, or was there someone to do that for you?" Kent slipped the bridle on the mare. Securing it, he spread a blanket over her back.

"There was someone to do it for me." He didn't

have to turn around for her to know he was sneering. "But I still did it myself."

Without waiting for him to deliver a snide comment, Brianne moved past Kent and into the stall. All her fears about him giving her an ornery horse vanished. The dapple-gray had the gentlest eyes she'd ever seen.

"Oh, aren't you a beauty?" Taken, she slowly stroked the silky muzzle. Brianne glanced at the hindquarters to ascertain the horse's gender before asking, "What's her name?"

"Skye." His eyes narrowed as Brianne fished two white lumps out of her pocket and held them in the palm of her hand. "You brought sugar?"

Skye gobbled up the evidence before he finished his question. Brianne laughed and patted the horse. "I always believe in bringing a bribe along." She glanced at him. "Helps smooth the road."

He didn't care for the implications of that, but somehow, Kent couldn't quite get himself to frown at her. Had to be something in the breakfast she'd fixed him. "Like coffee?"

She could almost make the innocent look on her face work, Kent thought. He tried not to be affected as he watched her lay her cheek against Skye's muzzle. If he didn't know any better, he would have sworn that Brianne was a country girl, born and raised.

"I plead the fifth."

Kent snorted. Turning his back on her, he went to get the saddles. "You can plead all you want and bribe all you want, I don't intend to make it easy on you."

Brianne liked honesty. Honesty was easier to deal with than lies that came in fancy packages. Honesty meant that there were no uncomfortable surprises to deal with later.

"I never asked you to," she reminded him. She followed behind him, meaning to fetch her own saddle. She wasn't going to give him any excuse to say that she wasn't pulling her own weight. "If I can feel the aches, I can write about them."

He deliberately avoided looking in her direction. Instead, he carried her saddle over to Skye and set it on top of the blanket. "Fair enough."

In the midst of all the commotion, later that afternoon, with the fire crackling near him and the calf lowing before him, Kent stopped and looked over his shoulder at Brianne. She was dirty, undoubtedly sweaty, and there was a streak of soot along her cheek that somehow managed to make her look better, not worse. For all that, she still looked sexy as hell.

Though it didn't come easy, he had to give her credit. She'd endured it all without a single word of complaint.

He figured she would cut out long before now, but she'd stuck, like one of those round little labels they insisted on sticking on apples these days. Stuck fast and hard.

Turning back around again, Kent waited until the

branding iron turned red-hot. On the ground in front
of him was one of the new calves he and his men—
and Brianne—had rounded up. The sound it was uttering was pitiful.

He'd expected Brianne to say something about
how barbaric branding was, or at least turn several
shades of green the first time she saw the iron meet
flesh and heard the brief, distinctive sizzle. She did
neither. Instead, she had withstood it all, snapping
away with that infernal camera of hers and keeping
up, even when the pace had gotten hectic. Rounding
up the last bunch had been particularly difficult.

"Achy enough?" he asked.

Brianne glanced up from her viewfinder. Was he
talking to her or one of his men? "What?"

"You said if you felt the aches, you could write
about them," he reminded her. "I asked you if you
were achy enough."

Brianne laughed under her breath, surprised that
he'd remember that. Surprised that he actually remembered anything she'd said. She raised her camera again.

"I'm getting there."

Denying that she was beginning to ache would
have been a lie and they both knew it. There were
parts of her anatomy that were going to hate her for
this come tomorrow morning. Parts that even now
were starting to throb. She couldn't remember riding
this hard on any of the other ranches she'd visited.
While her other subjects had gone out of their way

to make ranching seem easier, more modern, Kent had gone out of his way to do just the opposite.

Ranching was hard work, she'd never doubted it. With him as her guide, she saw that it could be positively grueling.

She knew he was trying to make her give up, cry uncle and put away her camera as she retreated. Maybe it was a guy thing, she didn't know, but whatever was motivating him, she wasn't about to let it get the better of her. She enjoyed the challenge of keeping up. More than that, she was going to enjoy proving him wrong. She wasn't one of those soft people he sneered at. And anyway, this was actually rather enjoyable for her. After spending so much time in the city, she welcomed the spaciousness she found out here.

Kent couldn't help being aware of her. He looked at her for a second. The hat she'd worn was on her back now, and her hair, gleaming like spun gold in the sun, kept falling into her eyes. Why did pushing it back for her seem so inviting? She was making his mind wander, he realized, annoyed with himself.

"Hold her down!" Kent ordered gruffly.

Brianne had the uncomfortable feeling he meant her, until the hired hands around him crowded in to still the calf. Through the eye of the camera, she watched as Kent pressed the hot metal to the animal's flank. The smell was horrid. Though she didn't wince, Brianne doubted she'd ever forget it.

It might even keep her from ordering a steak next time around.

Brianne lowered her camera and turned away, slowly dragging air into her lungs. Not that she'd ever tell Kent, she thought. He'd take the fact that she was affected as a sign of weakness.

She didn't have to be told that he had no patience with any displays of weakness. Strength was the only thing he respected. As long as she had to rely on Kent's good graces, she intended to garner his respect.

Feeling better, she raised the camera again. Adjusting the lens, she shot several more photographs, capturing the scene in three different formats. She used close-ups to take in the details, regular shots to take in a standard view of the scene and panoramic shots to help fuel the romance that still clung to the land and the legend.

Lowering her camera, she smiled in satisfaction. Her body might feel as if it had been ground up and spit out, but her work was going well.

Finished, Kent sprang to his feet and out of the way. The calf, still lowing pitifully, bucked beneath the hands that were holding her down.

"Let her go, boys."

With the restraints gone, the calf immediately staggered to its feet. The next moment, it ran for its mother, making the most of its freedom.

Kent let the branding iron fall on the ground. "Well, that's the last of them for today." He walked over to Brianne. He kept a close eye on her camera. So far, he'd caught her aiming that thing at him eight times. That was eight more than he was happy about.

Not sure what prompted him to do it, he reached over and ran his thumb over her cheek, wiping away the soot mark. On a stack of Bibles, he wouldn't have been able to explain why he felt something tighten inside of him. He shoved his hands into his back pockets.

"Want me to take you back?"

Brianne ran her hand over her cheek before answering. She could still feel the imprint of his thumb. Odd that such a rough movement could feel so gentle. There was more to this man than he'd like to admit, she mused.

If he put the question to her that way, it meant he wasn't planning on taking the rest of the day off himself. She wanted no special treatment. The deal was to follow him around from dawn to dusk.

"No," she answered. "I don't. What else is on your schedule for today?"

He might have known it wasn't going to be easy getting rid of her. Okay, she asked for it. "There's a length of fence we have to finish mending."

We. He really didn't believe in letting others do his work for him. She liked that.

"Fine." Brianne put the lens cap on her camera. "I'll come along."

"I was afraid you'd say that," he muttered, shaking his head.

Kent heard some of his men snicker behind him. They all seemed to like having her around. Since he'd brought her with him and introduced her around, all of them had been behaving like a bunch of bumbling adolescents. He'd caught his foreman,

Jack Russell, almost preening in front of her. And he was getting married in a week. Some of the others actually stopped what they were doing and posed for her, when they weren't hamming it up.

And when she asked them to line up for a group shot, they'd practically fallen over each other to oblige. You would have thought that there was some kind of prize being awarded at the end of the day.

Well, maybe they wanted to get her attention, but he sure as hell didn't. The more they tried to please her, the harder he was on her. He still hadn't quite figured out why he reacted that way, but he saw no reason to burden himself with the puzzle. Most likely it was because he saw her as a damn nuisance and nothing more complicated than that.

He frowned at her as he mounted his horse. "I can still take you back. Last chance."

Swinging into the saddle, Brianne looked at him before answering, her eyes holding his. He had the uncomfortable feeling she was looking right through him.

And then she shook her head. "Not the way I see it."

He had no idea what she meant by that, but he figured he was better off not asking. Talking to women only led to trouble.

Just look at the way his men were behaving. A bunch of grown men, performing like trained bears. Damn pitiful, if you asked him.

"C'mon then," he muttered. "We're burning daylight." Kicking his heels against Whiskey's flanks, he galloped off.

4

When he heard the front door open and then close, Quint looked up from the newspaper he was reading. He'd dropped by his parents' house, curious to see the woman who, according to Will's story, had their brother so bent out of joint.

What he saw was one very shapely, slightly dusty-looking lady. She had hair the color of corn just kissed by the sun and had to be, despite the fact that she looked exceeding tired, one of the handsomest women he'd ever seen.

He smiled a greeting when their eyes met. "You look like someone rode you hard and put you away wet."

Brianne didn't know him, but he looked enough like Kent and Will for her to guess that he had to be yet another brother. His features were a little more chiseled, his hair a little darker blond and longer, but he was a Cutler, through and through, no doubt about it. Instead of an answer, a sigh escaped her dry lips. With a sense of longing, she contemplated the sofa, but knew that if she sat down now, chances were she wouldn't be able to get up. Not for hours.

By her reckoning, there was only so much energy left in her body and she had to use it wisely. Getting up the stairs to her room was going to be all the challenge she figured she could safely face.

Company or not, she couldn't stand having her shirt stick to her ribs any longer. She pulled her shirt-tails out from the waistband of her equally sweaty jeans, then held the shirt away from her. Anything to feel a little air.

Only then could she muster a smile. Rode hard and put away wet, huh? That about fit the bill. "I think they did."

Rising, he crossed to her. He was immediately taken by her eyes. Quint had always believed you could tell a lot about a person by their eyes. Hers were bright and lively. And beautiful. That matched what Will had told him.

"Hi, I'm Quint."

"The second oldest," she remembered, shaking the hand he extended to her. "I figure you already know I'm Brianne Gainsborough." News traveled fast in small towns and even faster between family members. Unless, of course, one of those members was Kent. She got the impression that if it were up to Kent, she'd remain a secret no one knew about.

"Yeah." Quint let his gaze slide over her appreciatively. Nice packaging, he mused. There, too, he agreed with Will. He had no idea what was wrong with their younger brother. "Kent giving you a rough time?"

She tried to rotate her shoulders and felt a twinge

of pain starting between her shoulder blades. Every place on her body either ached, or was beginning to. And it would be worse tomorrow. She wasn't looking forward to morning. "He probably doesn't think so."

Quint knew how pigheaded Kent could be. His brother had mostly steered clear of all females, save their mother and Morgan, ever since Rosemary Taylor had done her number on his heart. Knowing Kent, he probably lumped Brianne in with the likes of the Taylor woman.

"I'll talk to him," he promised.

"No." Brianne realized she'd shouted the protest, but the last thing she wanted was for Kent's big brother to lecture him on her behalf. She didn't need anyone interceding for her. This was something she'd handle on her own.

She flashed an apologetic smile and shaved some of the agitation from her voice. "It's all right. I don't want special treatment. I told Kent that I just want to be invisible."

Now that was downright impossible. A rumble of a laugh dismissed the very notion. "From where I'm standing, the only way that's going to happen is if you leave or turn into one of the head of cattle."

Her appreciation was in her eyes. "Thanks, I needed that."

With a gait that she knew was less than graceful, she made her way toward the winding staircase.

He noticed that she was limping. Kent probably

kept her in the saddle for most of the day. "Anything I can do for you?"

Brianne couldn't summon the energy to look over her shoulder at him. Besides, she was afraid that if she did she would fall over. "Short of carrying me up the stairs, you can tell me where the liniment is."

With a feeling of triumph, she put her hand out to capture the banister. *Almost there.*

Quint laughed. "I can do both." The next moment, he very carefully, very gently swept her up in his arms.

Surprised, Brianne tried to protest, but her heart really wasn't in it. "Wait, I didn't mean—"

He ignored her feeble protest. "In case no one's told you, I'm the sheriff. It's my job to make sure that the people in and around Serendipity stay safe." He saw her brows draw together in confusion. "If I let you go up those stairs in your condition, I'd be guilty of negligence. You might fall and break that pretty neck of yours. Now, we just can't have that happening." He winked at her. "Not even to a photojournalist."

It felt like heaven, being off her feet, but she didn't feel right about letting him carry her up the stairs like this.

"But—"

He wasn't about to let her try to talk him out of it. He'd managed heavier loads than her just helping out on the ranch.

Slowly, careful not to jostle her, Quint began to make his way up the stairs. Since according to what

Will had told him she was a reasonable sort, he pretended to appeal to her common sense.

"Think of it as a favor to me. I'd be stuck filling out all those reports." In a slow drawl, he enumerated the complications. "Then your father would want to know what happened and the paper would send in reporters." He shook his head. "Too much of a hassle." He drew her a tad closer, savoring the feel of the lady. "Carrying you up the stairs is a hell of a lot easier."

She knew when to give up. Especially when surrendering felt so good. "If you say so."

Quint took his time. The stairs were wide and the load a pleasant one. "I surely do say so."

Brianne slipped one arm around his neck. Now why couldn't Kent be like this? "I guess you're the one who got the manners."

A hint of the fierce family loyalty that existed in all of them surfaced. "We've all got manners, Brianne." Still, loyalty or not, he knew Kent's shortcomings. "Some of us just don't want to show them, that's all." He shrugged. "Afraid of using them up, I guess."

No danger of that in Kent's case, Brianne thought. "Is Kent always so hard on women, or am I special?"

"He is, *and* you're special." Quint grinned, looking down at her. "Kent's a good guy, but he doesn't venture out of his shell much. The one time I know of that he did, he got his heart stomped on. Messed up his people skills something awful."

"My people skills are just fine and what the hell do you think you're doing?"

Turning slightly, Quint looked down. Kent was at the bottom of the stairs, glaring up at him. "Taking what's left of this fine young woman and bringing her up to her room." Quint gave his brother a reproving look. "You ought to be ashamed, Kent."

Against his better judgment, Kent had turned his horse around after he'd left Brianne and ridden back to the house. He thought to perhaps mumble half an apology—not that she had one coming, but he had to admit she'd tried really hard to keep up. He figured effort deserved some sort of recognition.

But any notions of an apology had evaporated in the heat that overtook him when he saw her in his older brother's arms.

First his father, then the hands, now Quint. What was it with this woman? Did she get some sort of perverse pleasure out of seeing how many men she could wrap around her finger?

Kent blew out a breath as he took the stairs two at a time until he stood one step shy of the one they were on. Ignoring Brianne, he looked at Quint. "What I ought to be is having my head examined for letting everyone talk me into this."

Quint snorted. "Now that's a crock and you know it. Nobody's ever been able to talk you into anything you didn't want to do since you were old enough to talk. Everybody knows you've got a head like a rock."

This sounded like the makings of an argument and

Brianne didn't relish literally hanging between them at a time like that. She tapped Quint on his shoulder because he seemed to have forgotten that he was still holding her.

"Excuse me, but maybe you'd better put me down before you drop me."

This time, there was a trace of wickedness in the grin Quint aimed her way. "Not likely."

Kent scowled. He'd heard just about enough. "Give her here, she's my responsibility."

Nice to see him coming around, Quint thought. He had a good feeling about these two. Brianne, with her outgoing way, was just what his brooding brother needed in his life. "Whatever you say." He began to hand Brianne over to his brother.

What was she, a package of ground beef? Brianne braced her hand against Kent's chest before he had a chance to take her from Quint.

"Now hold it, I am no one's responsibility but my own." It was as if she hadn't said a word. Quint completed the transfer. Brianne could feel her temper threatening to flare as Kent took her. "And I am not a 'thing' to be passed back and forth," she added, struggling not to sound as annoyed as she was.

"Not a thing, more like a hot potato," Kent told her matter-of-factly. She weighed less than a guilty conscience, he noted. "Now stop wiggling, or we'll both fall down the stairs."

If he used that half of a brain he had, Brianne thought, he would have realized that she wasn't wiggling. Any motion he felt was just the aftermath of her being passed into his arms. But there was no reasoning with him. Resigning herself, Brianne laced her arms around his neck. This way, if he "accidentally" dropped her, she'd take him with her.

She studied the dark look on his face. "Well, it's a cinch you're not about to win the Mr. Congeniality award any time soon."

Kent kept his mind on the stairs and not on the woman pressed up against him. It was a whole lot simpler that way. He wasn't much good at complications when it came to women. He was still trying to figure out why he'd grabbed her from Quint like that. It wasn't like him. That, too, had to be her fault.

"Not after any award," he muttered, not even sure what it was she was babbling about.

"Good, then you won't be disappointed."

He stopped. The look he leveled at her had silenced a man twice her size, but he had a feeling it would have no effect on her. Woman probably didn't have the sense she was born with. "Whether or not I'm disappointed about anything is no concern of yours."

Ouch. He'd certainly put her in her place. Not that Brianne had expected to mean anything to him, but being told as much had a certain sting to it she didn't care for. She was accustomed to people liking her, not going after her scalp.

"Well, that was refreshingly honest." There was no reason for him to be this nasty to her. She hadn't done anything to him. On the contrary, she'd gone out of her way to be pleasant when he was downright surly. "Tell me, just what put the bur under your saddle, Kent?"

He answered before he could think better of it. "You, for one." With his elbow, he eased open the door that was standing ajar. Shifting her slightly, he walked into her room.

"Why? I didn't get in the way today. I even helped," Brianne reminded him.

She'd herded cattle, helped cut the calves out and then gone on to help work on the length of fence that needed mending. She was bowlegged, dirty, tired and had scratches along her left arm where the barbed wire had gone through her jacket. Just what did she have to do to win this man over?

He was talking too much and he knew it, but Kent couldn't seem to stop. "The only way you could have helped today was to get a bag and put yourself in it. You were a distraction, lady. To everyone."

To everyone. That had to include him. It hadn't been his intention to make the rebuke sound like a compliment, but she took it that way. Surprise widened her eyes as she looked at him.

"Everyone?"

"Yeah, everyone." Reaching her bed, Kent dropped her on top of the comforter, as if to punish her for what he was thinking right now. For what he wanted to do right now.

Brianne tried very hard not to wince as she felt her body jar. "I distracted you," she said very slowly, digesting the meaning behind his words, unintentional or not.

He knew he should be going, but somehow, he couldn't get his feet to work. They remained there, in front of her bed, immobilized by some unknown force. The leash on his temper was shortening.

"Isn't that what I just said?"

Brianne rose to her knees on the edge of the bed, her aches and pains forgotten, at least for the moment. "Why?"

Why. The woman wanted to know why. Next, she'd be asking for a pound of his flesh. "Because you kept talking and snapping that camera of yours." But that wasn't the main reason and he had a feeling that she knew it. "And because you kept smelling of honeysuckle."

All the fight had gone out of her, to be replaced by a warm smile. "Oh?"

"And you kept doing that." He jerked his head at her. At her expression. "You kept smirking."

He was floundering and he knew it, Brianne thought. "That's not a smirk, that's a smile," she contradicted softly.

"Same thing," he bit off. Damn it, why wasn't he leaving? Why was he standing here, looking at her as if he was some feebleminded lapdog, longing for a very particular lap? Maybe his sister Morgan was right after all. Maybe he needed a night on the town just to get rid of this strange, charged energy that was battering him. He needed a woman, any woman.

Any woman but her.

There hadn't been any energy battering at him until Brianne had showed up, he reminded himself. Kent chalked up another strike against her.

"No, it's not." She drew closer. Too close for Kent's comfort.

"With a smirk, one side of your mouth goes up. With a smile, you use both lips and they curve on both ends." He could feel her breath along his face as she spoke. Kent began to feel itchy. Itchy in a way he knew he couldn't scratch.

"Like this." Brianne smiled up at him. "See?"

He saw. He saw all right. He saw that he had one hell of a major problem on his hands. A problem he damn well could do without.

A problem that was going to be his, nonetheless. Swearing, Kent was barely aware of what he did next, only what followed after that. Vaguely, he recalled taking her by the shoulders and pulling her toward him instead of away. The desperate thought burrowed its way into his brain that since he couldn't get her to back off by working her hard, maybe he could do it by scaring her.

She sure as hell was scaring him.

His mouth came down on hers, quickly, urgently, like an eagle swooping down on its prey before it got away. Taking what he'd been thinking about ever since she'd kissed him yesterday.

Even after a day in the saddle, she still tasted like sugar-dusted strawberries.

And he still had a craving for sugar-dusted strawberries. Worse than ever.

The air had whooshed out of Brianne the instant

he'd pulled her to him. Now she felt as if she had leaped into the center of a roaring fire, barefoot up to her neck. She was consumed by it. By him.

Heat wrapped itself around her as tightly as a tourniquet. She anchored herself to the overwhelming sensation he created within her by lacing her arms along his neck.

A muffled moan escaped as she struggled to hold her own in this. Struggled not to be swept away and burnt to a cinder.

If Kent meant to frighten her away, he succeeded only in frightening himself. Frightening himself because of the intensity that she somehow managed to drag out of him. Frightening himself because of the degree of passion she seemed to have unearthed. Passion he hadn't even realized existed.

Very slowly, he drew her arms away from his neck and moved back on shaky legs. What was it that she did to him? It almost didn't feel real. "Maybe you'd better stop smiling for a while."

Right now, Brianne wasn't sure if she had sufficient lip power to manage a smile, even a weak one. She sank down on the bed, completely boneless.

He berated her, made her jump through hoops and then kissed her until she felt raw inside. Brianne shook her head. "You are one hard man to figure out."

Finally beginning to recover, Kent started edging out of the room. "Then don't try."

"But it's my job," Brianne protested. And now, maybe her calling, she added silently, because she wanted to know more things about Kent Cutler than what went into a lengthy article with glossy pages.

"Get a new one," Kent shot back. Turning, he walked straight into his brother, who was in the doorway. How long had he been there? From the grin on his face, Kent guessed too long.

Kent scowled at him. Why hadn't Quint left yet? What was he doing here, anyway? "Don't you have a town to protect, or a Wanted poster to hang up?"

Quint held up the bottle of liniment he'd gone to fetch. It tickled him to see the way his brother was behaving. If he didn't miss his guess, Brianne Gainsborough had it all over that annoying Taylor girl who had set his brother mooning and brooding.

"Just bringing the lady what she requested." Quint elbowed past his younger brother.

Annoyed, Kent snatched the bottle from Quint's hand. The words on the label registered. He raised a brow as he turned around to look at Brianne. "So you're sore."

He said it as if he'd won some kind of silent bet. She felt herself bristling. "God would be sore after a day like today."

Kent raised a shoulder and let it drop carelessly. "I'm not."

"Then you're one up on God," Brianne said sweetly. With effort, she swung her legs off the bed. At least he was good for one thing, she thought. He made her so angry, she forgot to be exhausted. The soul of determination, she crossed to him, her hand out. "Now, if you don't mind," she began, tugging at the bottle, he wouldn't release it, "I'd like to put this on in private."

Kent had seen the way she'd hunched her shoulders on the way back. Seen the way she'd rotated them. Unless she was incredibly double-jointed, the liniment wasn't going to do her any good. "You're not going to be able to put it on where it hurts."

She raised her eyes to his, the comment, ripe and pregnant, hanging between them. "Can you?" she asked significantly.

Atta girl, Quint thought, mentally applauding her. If his brother let this one slip by, he was going to disavow any relation to him, Quint promised silently.

Very quietly, he let himself out of the room, easing the door shut behind him.

Still holding on to the bottle, Kent gestured toward the bed. "Just turn around, sit on the bed and pull up your shirt."

He caught her by surprise, but she managed to recover quickly. "Why Kent, we hardly know one another," she teased, fluttering her lashes at him.

He wasn't sure if she was laughing at him or not, but he wasn't taking any chances. "What, you don't think I know what the back of a bra looks like?" He'd gotten her in this condition, he might as well do something about getting her out of it. That attempting to do so was in direct contradiction of his plan was something he chose not to think about right now.

The smile she gave him was nothing short of

wicked. "You might know what the back of one looks like, but I'm not wearing one."

The bottle met the top of the bureau with a resounding whack as he all but dropped it. Kent wasn't about to take on any more temptation than he felt he could safely handle.

"I'll get my mother," Kent said just before he disappeared.

He hated the fact that the laughter that followed him from Brianne's room was at his expense. Hated even more that all he'd wanted to do was to remain in the room and apply the liniment himself.

But some things, he knew, were best left alone. This was definitely one of them.

It got easier.

After a couple of days, her body began to get accustomed to the hard pace she'd found herself maintaining. Or rather, that Kent had her maintaining. After the dust had settled from their initial sparring, she realized that the pace he kept up was his usual one. And that was, after all, what she'd asked for at the start. To observe what it was really like to run the Shady Lady, follow the itinerary of a real working cowboy. It was her intent to be part of the daily grind that went into running a ranch, and yet find the beauty in it.

To her credit, she thought she was accomplishing both rather well. It helped that she was enjoying herself. She began to understand the sense of satisfaction that went with a good day's work out here. More than that, she was beginning to feel that satisfaction, too.

She had the feeling that even Kent couldn't really find fault with her efforts. Oh, she was a long way off from making Rancher of the Year, but she was definitely not the liability he'd obviously been afraid she'd be.

The only thing that was missing was hearing him admit it.

But that, she knew, was something that was not about to happen any time soon. Kent Cutler wasn't the type to admit he was wrong about something, especially a female. Well, he was going to admit it about this female. He just didn't know it yet. Brianne smiled to herself. She was going to enjoy making him come around. It was a matter of pride...and maybe a little something more.

"So how is it going?" Jake prodded over dinner at the end of Brianne's first week.

He accepted the bowl of potatoes his wife passed him and gave himself a generous helping before passing it along to his son. He waited for Kent, there by Zoe's mandate, to answer.

But it was Brianne who responded first. She slanted a glance toward Kent as she said, "Great."

It was in fact, Kent thought, going better than he had first anticipated. Everything he threw at her, she bore up to. Any other woman, with the possible exception of Morgan who had a wicked stubborn streak, would have given up by now. But Brianne just dug in. In addition, she seemed to be entirely without vanity, entirely without a threshold over which she would not venture.

Ranching was obviously not her way of life, yet she wouldn't knuckle under. More than that, she was ready for every day with that damn smile on her face and that look of enthusiasm in her eyes.

She obviously had no common sense, he concluded.

"Could be worse," Kent muttered. He drowned the mashed potatoes in gravy.

"Kent."

There was a sharp warning note in Zoe's voice. He might be a man in a great many ways, but there was still that headstrong little boy in him. The one who refused to cry uncle. He'd been the sickly one when he was little. And there'd been that winter old-timers still talked about, the winter when Kent had been so sick and she'd been so afraid that she would lose him. But he had hung on, a tiny boy of three, too stubborn to do anything else. Then his stubbornness had saved his life. Now, Zoe feared, it threatened to ruin it.

Brianne didn't want dinner disrupted because Kent couldn't bring himself to say that she'd held up her end. "That's all right, Zoe. Kent is obviously the type who's slow in coming around."

The look in his blue eyes when he raised them to her face stopped her breath for a long moment. "I'm not slow."

Well, at least he was directing his conversation

toward her for a change. This last day, everything he'd said that was intended for her had come through someone else. She had no idea what she'd done to offend him—except keep up.

"I didn't say you were slow, I said you were slow in coming around. There is a difference." As she spoke, she could feel her temper heating, getting the better of her even as she told herself to back away. "What you don't seem to appreciate is that there're many shades to things. Nothing is black or white. And people don't fall into categories."

She had some nerve, lecturing him in his parents' house, the house that he'd grown up in. Even more of a nerve, considering what she was about.

He laid his fork down. "Isn't that what you're doing? Sticking me into a damn category for your readers' amusement?" His mouth twisted in contempt. "'See the cowboy. See him ride. See him rope. Watch him do tricks.'"

"Watch him make a damn fool of himself because he can't admit he's wrong." That had come out before Brianne could stop it. Embarrassed, annoyed at Kent for making her break one of her cardinal rules about decorum, Brianne rose. "I'm sorry," she apologized to his parents. "My father always said my mouth would get me into trouble."

Amen to that, Kent thought.

Had it been him in her place, Jake thought, he would have clipped Kent a long time ago. "Don't be," he told her. "Until this second, I wasn't altogether sure you were Brian's girl. He got hot under the collar a lot more than you with a lot less provocation.'' He looked pointedly at his son.

She was grateful for Jake's understanding, but that didn't excuse her. "Still, this is your house and I shouldn't be sitting here, insulting your son.''

"By all means, insult him,'' Zoe urged her. "Maybe it'll do him some good. You're not saying anything he doesn't deserve. Is she, Kent?'' Zoe looked at her middle child.

"Whatever you say, Ma.'' Kent retired his knife and fork, hardly having touched anything. "If you'll excuse me, I've suddenly lost my appetite.'' Leaving his napkin on the table, Kent walked out.

5

It took Jake a moment to realize that Kent was actually walking out. His son had a few rough edges, but Jake couldn't remember Kent ever being downright rude before. He wasn't about to stand for it in his own home, especially not in front of the daughter of one of his oldest friends.

"Damn it, Kent, you come back here. Do you hear me?" Jake called after him.

The sound of the front door slamming was his only answer. Disgusted, Jake threw his own napkin on the table, ready to storm after Kent and drag him into the house. Anger colored his cheeks.

"I'll bring him back," he promised Brianne. "He's not so old that he can't show a little respect—"

Brianne placed a gently restraining hand on Jake's arm, drawing his attention momentarily away from the center of his anger.

"This is my fault, Jake." She felt terrible about the scene. "Please, let me go talk to him."

Jake was torn for a moment. He didn't think that anything Brianne had to say would make a dent in

Kent's thick hide. Still, he didn't intend to stand in her way if she felt she had to go after Kent.

With a reluctant sigh, he gestured toward the door. "All right, but if he gets ugly, just give a yell."

With a smile, Brianne paused only to brush her lips over the older man's cheek. She appreciated the concern. Except for Kent, the Cutler men all seemed to be sweet. "Don't worry, I've seen him at his worst. I can handle him."

Maybe she could, at that. All the same, Jake shook his head as he watched his guest leave. What was the matter with Kent? Here was a beautiful, unattached woman practically gift-wrapped on his doorstep and instead of making the most of the situation, Kent was behaving as if he'd come face-to-face with a king-size diamondback.

Baffled, Jake sat down at the table again. "I don't know what's gotten into him."

Zoe waited until she heard the front door close and Brianne was gone. "I do."

"Well then, please. Enlighten me."

Zoe laughed softly as she covered the hand of the man she had shared her bed and her life with for the last thirty-some years. He could be so blind sometimes.

Jake would have resented the laughter at his expense if he didn't love her so much.

"Oh darlin', if I haven't managed to open your eyes in the last thirty-four years, one little conversation now isn't going to make a difference." Leaning over, Zoe gently smoothed the frown forming on his lips in response to her words with her fingertips. "You never could see what was right there in front of you."

He knew it was useless to argue. Zoe had an insight into things that he couldn't even begin to understand. That was one of the reasons he loved her. To him, she was still the young, laughing-eyed girl he had fallen so hard for that first year in college. The year his life had begun.

Jake pressed her hand to his lips, kissing it softly. "I saw you, didn't I?"

He still thought he was the one who had made the first move. It just went to prove her point. Zoe stroked his hair, hair still as thick, as golden as his sons'. "Only after I practically bent your neck to make you take a look."

A hint of the scowl that had so often graced Kent's face this last week whispered along Jake's face. This rang no bells. "How?"

Zoe's eyes were bright with amusement as she looked at the man who still was, after all this time, the center of her universe. "You think it was coincidence that I was there every day at the café when you came by at three with your friends?"

He'd always believed it was his good fortune that fate had placed her there. "Wasn't it?"

Zoe tried not to laugh. The expression on Jake's face was nothing short of amazed as he contemplated the contrary.

"That's what I love about you, Jake, you're still so innocent when it comes to the ways of women."

After all this time, there was no harm in the truth coming out. She would have told him sooner if the subject had come up. "I had my cousin Alice pump your brother for information."

Jake digested the import of the words. He'd suspected as much, but never said anything for fear that it had merely been his manly pride prompting the notion. So, he'd been right all along. With an oath, he tugged Zoe from her chair onto his lap.

As she laughed, he nuzzled her neck. After all these years, she still smelled of lavender. He'd always had a weakness for lavender. Just as he'd always had a weakness for her.

"Do you mean to tell me that I married a devious woman?"

"You betcha." The laughter faded from her lips as she brought her mouth down to his. She hoped Brianne wouldn't be returning too soon.

Brianne had fully expected to have to go running after Kent, but she found him standing on the other side of the porch, staring at the sky. Maybe he wasn't leaving, just wanted some time to cool off.

She came up behind him quietly, some of the fire within her breast dying down. His shoulders were so rigid, she debated whether she should approach him at all. But she had nothing to lose. He'd already bitten her head off several times over. And the thought of walking back in and facing the Cutlers without him was not an option for her.

"There was no reason for you to leave the table like that."

Kent had been lost in thought, and he started, surprised that she'd followed him out. Didn't the woman *ever* know when to back off?

Maybe he shouldn't be so surprised, he silently amended, turning his head to give her a look calculated to make her keep her distance.

"Yes, there was." His voice was cold, detached. "I lost my appetite."

If he thought she was going to turn tail and retreat just because he wore an expression that could have turned some that she knew to stone, he was sadly mistaken. "Because of me."

If she wasn't bright enough to figure that out, he wasn't going to hand her the answer. Instead, he turned away again, leaning back against the railing. He stared up at the stars again. Tranquility refused to come. He hadn't felt at peace since she had arrived. Another reason to send her on her way.

"Maybe."

Well, if he wasn't going to look at her, she damn well was going to get in his face. Circling, Brianne confronted him. "Why do I irritate you so much?"

His eyes narrowed. Why was she asking the obvious? "Because you do." He turned away again.

Refusing to be ignored, she planted herself in front of him a second time. Two could play at this damn game all night if that was what he wanted. "That's not much of an answer."

This time he didn't bother looking away. "It's the only one you're getting."

She felt like shaking him. Getting him to talk was like trying to get a block to roll. And getting him to admit to the obvious electricity that was buzzing between them was twice as difficult as that. Why couldn't he just enjoy it for the short length of time she was going to be here instead of throwing up roadblocks?

Shifting her approach in mid-gear, she smiled knowingly. "But there is another one, right?"

The woman had a smile that went straight to his gut. Irritated as well as drawn, Kent moved away from her. It was time he left. God only knew why he hadn't gotten on his horse already.

"There's part of it right there."

She wasn't sure what he meant, only that there was something there that was stronger than the anger. Moving quickly, she darted in front of him. He was going to stay and finish this conversation even if she had to hog-tie him with one of those fancy knots the wranglers had taught her.

"What is?"

"You won't let anything go at face value. You've got to dig at it, turn it around, take a picture of it from all angles until you've stripped it clean." He realized he was shouting and lowered his voice. She set him off faster than the cherry bombs he and Morgan used to explode every Fourth of July as kids.

Was that how he saw it? Brianne wondered. That she stripped things, like some conscienceless scavenger? The thought bitterly disappointed her. "I don't strip anything clean, I make it clear. I try to understand it so that other people can appreciate it for themselves. Like the beauty in the solitude of what you do rather than the loneliness."

He didn't hold with exploring things. Thinking things too deep always got you into trouble. Thinking made him realize how golden her hair was, how soft her skin was. How alive he felt, kissing her. Trouble, that's all thinking ever got you. Trouble with a capital *T*.

"The beauty in solitude is that it's just that, solitude." He glared at her, daring Brianne to shadow his movements. When she did, he knew he shouldn't have expected anything else. Why didn't she just take her damn camera and her damn scent and go home? She had already snapped enough photographs to fill a whole house full of magazines. "The beauty in Montana is that you can throw a rock without hitting seventeen people." He went toe-to-toe with her. If he couldn't walk away from her, he'd make her walk away from him. "You can throw it and not hit anyone at all."

He should have known better.

Brianne stood her ground, hands on hips, trying desperately to understand the man fate, with its warped sense of humor, was drawing her to.

"What are you afraid of? The readers aren't all going to hop the nearest plane and fly out here to settle down just because I write a section of an article on you and your precious little world."

He felt like wrapping his hands around her neck and squeezing.

Or wrapping his arms around her slim body and holding her to him.

Both would prove to be fatal mistakes.

Unable to successfully argue with her, he snapped, "I don't feel like sharing, all right?"

Her eyes searched his in the dim light coming from the house. "Montana, the ranch or your space?"

He paused for a moment, then answered honestly. "All three."

They weren't talking about anything so altruistic as the state or the ranch, she'd bet her soul on that. He was afraid, she realized. For some reason, he was afraid. Of her. "But mainly your space, right?"

"Right."

He'd fairly growled the admission in her face. It took everything she had not to step back. "I'm not sharing your space, Kent. I'm leasing it, for just another week. And then I'll be gone."

Gone. The single word echoed like a mournful hymn rising in air that was too hot to stir. "I know."

His expression was so strange, she couldn't begin to read it. "It's what you want, isn't it?"

"Yes," he bit off, as if by doing that, it could shield him from the rest of it. From all those other feelings he didn't want to deal with, didn't even want to acknowledge.

Brianne squared her shoulders, feeling as if she'd just been physically assaulted. Did he hate her being here that much? She tried to hide her hurt. "You know, if I didn't know better, I'd say that you said that just a little too fast with a little too much feeling in it."

Kent saw the hurt in her eyes, but did nothing to reach out to it. If he did, it would only draw her out more. And that would be his undoing.

He shrugged, indifferent. "It's because you guessed right."

This time, his voice, his expression, cut through her like a huge bowie knife. "Well, I guess that puts me in my place, doesn't it?" Pressing her lips together, she raised her chin. And tried to rally her scattered, wounded pride. "It's too late to try to line up someone else. I've got a deadline to meet." She'd never felt quite so lost before and didn't fully understand why. Or what to do about it. "But I'll make more of an effort to keep out of your way." Afraid the tension vibrating through her would release itself in tears, Brianne turned away.

She'd only taken a few steps toward the house before she heard him call her.

"Wait a minute."

As if his voice was an off switch, she stopped, still looking straight ahead of her. Brianne prayed neither of his parents would choose this moment to come out. She wasn't sure if she could carry on a coherent conversation. "What?"

"I'm not sure."

The strange, quiet note in his voice made her turn around to face him. "Not sure about what?"

He knew he shouldn't be saying it even as the words found their way out of his mouth. "Not sure if I want you to go."

Brianne stared at him incredulously. He was the most complicated so-called simple man she'd ever met. "What?"

Frustration had Kent saying more than he knew he should. "That's what's crawled under my skin, all right? The fact that I don't know if I want you to leave." He was stumbling over feelings that seemed so miserably tangled he was no longer certain which end was up. "That maybe there's a small part that wants you to stay, which is ridiculous because you are going." The look in his eyes challenged her to negate his statement. "Right?"

"Right." But her voice lacked any conviction as she agreed.

Kent blew out a breath, hating this ambivalence that was dogging him, haunting his thoughts. He didn't like complications. Complications only led to confusion, to a state he already knew he didn't function well in. He wasn't a slow learner. The incident with Rosemary had taught him that he should stick to what he understood. That did not include women. Even one who made his blood heat every time he looked at her.

He moved toward her, taking each step as if it were his last. "Another week, eh?"

Brianne swallowed. The air had stopped moving. Everything seemed still to her except for the beating of her heart. "That's all."

The half shrug that met her assurance was an attempt at carelessness. "I guess I can put up with it for another week." He kept his voice casual. "Where do you go from here?"

"Back to New York, to my office. I wasn't kidding about that deadline."

He could see her fitting well into an urbane world like that, taking in the theater, going to sophisticated restaurants where they served overpriced food and had long, convoluted conversations about things that didn't matter. Trouble was, he was beginning to see her fitting into his world as well. Beginning to want her to fit in. "I thought you said you don't live in New York."

"I don't. The magazine I work for is located in New York. I live in Connecticut."

"Connecticut." He'd never been very good in geography when it came to anything east of the Rockies besides the obvious states that everyone knew. Wasn't Connecticut some little bitty state north of New York?

She picked up on his tone. Didn't he think any place was worthy except for Montana? "You say that like it's a dread disease." Gamely, she interrupted their silent truce by asking, "What have you got against Connecticut?"

"Nothing, I just never thought about people living there, that's all." Certainly not people who lit up a dark Montana night with just a smile.

She wondered what he did think about, besides cattle. A smile born of the grudging affection she was beginning to develop for him rose to her lips. "Everybody's got to live somewhere, especially since you don't want them trespassing in Montana." She knew she was being defensive, but he was goading her into it. If she were honest with herself, she preferred what she saw right here to what she'd left behind. There was something so basic about life out here, basic, simple and beautiful. Or maybe it was just because he was here.

He straightened, bracing for something she didn't see. "You're doing it again."

Brianne didn't have a clue what he was talking about. "Doing what?"

He frowned, his eyes narrowing as he looked at her mouth despite the fact that common sense bid him not to. "Smirking."

She relaxed. "I told you before, that's smiling." Was he that unaccustomed to it? "I can't believe that women haven't smiled at you, Kent. Even though you do try to run them all off with a shotgun."

Just when he thought he was beginning to follow her, she lost him. "Now what are you talking about?"

"Well, you're not exactly hospitable. Quint told me that you're like that with all women."

"Quint?" A suspicion he was unaccustomed to feeling trickled through him, the same restlessness he felt when he saw her talking to his men out of earshot. "When did you see Quint?"

"Here, that second day. Don't you remember?"

"Oh. Yes, I do."

Kent felt more than a little foolish for jumping the gun. It was just that the thought of Quint seeking her out bothered him. The fact that it did bothered him even more. She was nothing to him, why did it matter to him whom she talked to? It just made no sense to him.

"Why, are you afraid I might taint the rest of your family if I talk to them?"

"No, I—" That wasn't it and she knew it. "Damn it, woman, you always twist everything around. Most of all, me."

He hadn't meant to say that. Kent could tell he made a mistake the moment he saw the look in her eyes.

"Meaning?"

Why did she want to play games? "You know what I mean."

Brianne drew closer to him. "If I knew, I wouldn't ask."

He could feel the heat of her body and struggled to keep from absorbing it in every fiber of his being. "You're a pest, you know that?"

"So you keep telling me." Her words were slow, drifting to him, lingering in the air between them. "I'm still trying to figure out what you mean by that."

"I mean that you keep getting in my way." Wasn't it enough that she'd messed with his mind? Wasn't she going to be satisfied until he spelled it all out for her?

Brianne thought of all the effort she'd put in to be

as unobtrusive as possible. The effort she'd put in to be a help rather than a hindrance. Why couldn't he just admit that? "I do not."

"Yes, you do. Up here—" he tapped his temple "—you get in my way up here."

A smile, warm and pleased, began to curl through her. They were getting there. By inches, but they were getting there. "How?"

"Just by being," he growled.

She looked up at him innocently, so close to him that if she were any closer, they would have been one. "I can't cease to be, Kent. At least, not for another week."

"That's just the problem."

How she had come to be in his arms like this, Kent hadn't the vaguest notion. All he knew was that she was there and he liked it far too much for it to be safe for him. He'd been down this road once before, a road he hadn't a single clue how to navigate.

No clue how to get from here to there. And in the middle was this huge hole. He'd already fallen through it once. He didn't want a repeat performance, not under any circumstances.

Yet he wasn't drawing his arms away, wasn't stepping back. Like a damn lemming, he remained on the path he was on.

Kent looked down into her face. "You know, women are a lot more complicated than cattle."

If she stayed really still, she could feel his heart beating. Hard, like hers. "I'll take that as a compliment."

"Wasn't meant to be."

Oh yes, it was. "Cutler?"

"Yeah?"

"Quit while you're ahead."

He framed her face with his hands. God, but he did want her. Wanted what was so bad for him. "Was I ahead?"

"Uh-huh." He was going to kiss her, she could see it in his eyes. Anticipation rushed through her veins. "But not as ahead as you're going to be."

When had his blood turned to fire like this? He hadn't even kissed her yet. "You do talk too much."

"So you said." She whispered the last word against his mouth as it came down on hers.

There was something wonderful about the familiarity of his kiss, something even more wonderful about the exhilaration it ushered in. Brianne wrapped her arms around his neck, leaning her body into his. Letting herself be taken away.

It was like riding a roller coaster in the dark. You thought you knew what was ahead, but you weren't altogether sure that someone hadn't changed the route on you when you weren't looking. So she went on the ride and held on for dear life, knowing only one thing. That when it was over, she was going to want it to begin all over again.

More, he wanted more, but more was just what Kent couldn't let himself have. He had to keep his goal in mind, to remain detached. She'd be gone in another week, and he could go back to life as he knew it. Dependable, stable.

And duller than rain on an endless prairie without her.

His arms closed around her again. It was hard to think of the future, hard to think of anything when white lightning was coursing through his veins.

She didn't taste like strawberries anymore. It was moonshine she brought to mind now. Moonshine far more potent than what he and Quint had sampled that time behind Joe Tyler's makeshift still.

Moonshine that had a kick he wasn't all that sure he could recover from.

With a shaky breath, Kent drew back just enough to look down into her face. Down at the mussed lips that had his imprint on them.

He tried to summon anger and found it was just beyond his reach. "Damn it, woman, where did you learn to kiss like that?"

There was mischief in her eyes. "Some things you don't learn. Some things just come naturally."

He wanted to believe that. Wanted to believe that there'd been no other men in her life, but he was no fool. There'd probably been a legion of them and he was just one of a number.

Suddenly, he wanted nothing more than to wipe the memory of all the others from her mind.

Murmuring an oath she couldn't quite make out, Kent kissed her again.

And again.

One kiss dovetailed into another, growing stronger, until they all melded into one huge, heated kaleidoscope that swirled through her head, making her dizzy with desire. Brianne felt she was going to climb out of her skin if he didn't make love with her tonight.

As if he could read her mind, Kent stopped suddenly. His heart pounding, throbbing in his ears, he took her hand without a word. Leading her to his horse, he got on, then extended his hand to her.

She debated, knowing that if she agreed, she was taking a very huge step. A step that might have consequences.

After a beat, she took the hand he offered and swung into the saddle behind him. With her arms tightly around his waist, Brianne held on as Kent turned Whiskey toward home.

His home.

6

————➤←————

Nerves skimmed along her body like ice skaters' blades along a freshly smoothed ice rink. Maybe she should have her head examined, feeling like this about a man who blew hot, then cold, but she couldn't quite help herself. There was something about the way he kissed her that completely undid her. Unlocked her soul like no one else ever had. She'd always believed in grabbing life with both hands. Excitement filled every space within her.

Brianne pressed her cheek against Kent's back. His warmth radiated through, heightening the anticipation churning within her. And at the center of it all was an enormous, baffling feeling of comfort. As if being here like this with Kent was where she'd always meant to be.

It was a silly notion, but silly or not, Brianne couldn't shake it.

Brianne raised her head to see where they were. Not that she had gotten any better at finding her way around this vast range in the last week than she had been at the outset. What she was hoping to see was a glimpse of Kent's house.

Squinting, she could just barely make it out. It would have been impossible to see at this distance, if not for the lights.

The entire house, from top to bottom, looked to be ablaze with lights.

Without being told, Brianne knew that wasn't like Kent. He wouldn't have just gone off and left all those lights on. She couldn't even visualize him turning on so many to begin with. He reminded her of someone who enjoyed the solitude that the dark offered. His electric bills were probably all in the single digits.

"Kent, you didn't leave a candle burning in every window, did you?"

Her breath, warm against his back, and the teasing question brought Kent back from the path where he'd strayed. His thoughts busy elsewhere, Kent hadn't been looking in front of him. Whiskey knew the way to the stable. Kent left it up to the horse to get them home.

His mind wasn't on getting home, but on what would happen once they'd gotten there. He was trying very hard not to think beyond the night ahead and the needs that were all but tearing his gut apart. For once, he didn't want to think about consequences.

Brianne's question was a fool question to ask. To him, a candle was something you used when the power went out. To her, it probably represented something romantic. He'd read that somewhere once.

Maybe tonight, he'd light one for her. But he certainly hadn't lit any earlier.

He half turned toward her. "No, I didn't."

She was right, he realized as he looked toward his house. There were lights on. Lots of lights. Any more and it would have looked as if the building was on fire. Even if he'd forgotten to turn off a light—which he hadn't, since when he'd left earlier it was still daylight—he'd never have turned all of them on. Why should he? He only occupied one room at a time.

"What the—?"

For a second, the sight baffled him. The realization that the rest of the evening was, at least temporarily, put on hold sank in a moment later. Frustrated, he swallowed an oath he figured was better left unsaid, given his present company.

Brianne felt Kent's body stiffen. "Do you think someone broke in?"

He laughed shortly. Robberies in and around Serendipity were few and very far in between. As a rule, drifters didn't come here and the townspeople didn't take from their own.

"Had to be one careless burglar to leave all the lights on."

No, it was worse than a burglar, he thought dourly. A burglar would have been in and out and long gone by now...without leaving the lights on. What this meant was that it had to be one of his family, paying a call.

But which one would turn on all the lights like

PLAY "LUCKY 7" AND GET
THREE FREE GIFTS!

HOW TO PLAY:

1. With a coin, carefully scratch off the silver box at the right. Then check the claim char to see what we have for you — **FREE BOOKS** and a gift — **ALL YOURS! ALL FREE!**

2. Send back this card and you'll receive brand-new Silhouette Yours Truly® novels. The books have a cover price of $3.50 each, but they are yours to keep absolutely free.

3. There's no catch. You're under no obligation to buy anything. We charge nothing — ZERO — for your first shipme And you don't have to make any minimum number of purchases — not even one!

4. The fact is thousands of readers enjoy receiving books by mail from the Silhouette Reader Service™ months before they're available in stores. They like the convenience o home delivery and they love our discount prices!

5. We hope that after receiving your free books you'll want to remain a subscriber. But the choice is yours — to continue or cancel, any time at all! So why not take us up on invitation, with no risk of any kind. You'll be glad you did!

YOURS FREE!

PLAY LUCKY 7 FOR THIS EXCITING FREE GIFT!

THIS SURPRISE MYSTERY GIFT COULD BE YOURS FREE WHEN YOU PLAY

LUCKY 7!

NO COST! NO OBLIGATION TO BUY!
NO PURCHASE NECESSARY!

PLAY THE

LUCKY 7 SLOT MACHINE GAME!

Just scratch off the silver box with a coin. Then check below to see the gifts you get!

YES!

I have scratched off the silver box. Please send me all the gifts for which I qualify. I understand I am under no obligation to purchase any books, as explained on the back and on the opposite page.

201 SDL CH5N
(U-SIL-YT-09/98)

Name
_____
PLEASE PRINT CLEARLY

Address _____ Apt.#

City _____ State _____ Zip _____

DETACH AND MAIL CARD TODAY!

The Silhouette Reader Service™ — Here's how it works

Accepting free books places you under no obligation to buy anything. You may keep the books and gift and return the shipping statement marked "cancel." If you do not cancel, about a month later we'll send you 4 additional novels, and bill you just $2.90 each, plus 25¢ delivery per book and applicable sales tax, if any.* That's the complete price — and compared to cover prices of $3.50 each — quite a bargain! You may cancel at any time, but if you choose to continue, every other month we'll send you 4 more books, which you may either purchase at the discount price...or return to us and cancel your subscription.

*Terms and prices subject to change without notice. Sales tax applicable in N.Y.

that? Even Morgan, who claimed to like things bright around her, didn't require having a light in every room.

By the time he pulled up in front of the house, Kent had his answer. There was a car parked in the driveway. A very familiar, albeit slightly dusty car.

He recognized it instantly. "Hank," he muttered under his breath.

His brother had moved to Southern California several months ago, looking to further his advertising career. Quick-witted, talented and enterprising, Hank'd long since outgrown the firm he'd been with and it had been just a matter of finding the right time to leave. They'd all believed that Hank was too good to waste his time and his talent going nowhere.

Though their paths hadn't crossed nearly as much as they used to since they'd reached manhood, Kent had to admit that there were times he found himself missing Hank and his perverse sense of humor.

According to their mother, Hank had been promising to come home for a visit for some time now. Truth be told, Kent had really been looking forward to seeing him.

Any time but now.

Kent shook his head. Damn, talk about bad timing.

Wondering if he could urge Hank off to the main house without arousing any undue suspicion, Kent dismounted. It took him a second to remember to offer his hand to Brianne.

"The burglar left his car," she observed, looking down at Kent. Obviously, he had to know whoever it was in his house. Brianne wondered if he could find a way to get rid of them.

"Yeah, I noticed."

His hands on her waist, Kent slowly lowered Brianne to the ground, allowing the length of her body to tease his. He could feel a quickening in his gut as well as his loins. There had to be a way to get rid of Hank.

The word *mistake* telegraphed itself through his brain, but Kent broke the connection. If this was a mistake, and it probably was, he'd deal with it later. Right now, he felt that if he couldn't have Brianne, and soon, he was going to self-destruct.

He'd muttered someone's name when he'd looked at the car, but Brianne hadn't made it out. "You know who's in your house?"

Kent nodded, making a detour around the vehicle and fighting the urge to kick all the tires. "Hank."

Brianne remembered the name. "Another brother." This was the one who had moved out of state. She tried to keep a tally in her head. "How many brothers did you say you had again?"

"Too many," he bit off. Taking her hand, Kent opened the front door and walked in. "Hank, come out and show your ugly face." No one answered. Puzzled, Kent looked around the narrow hallway. "What's with all the lights? When did you become afraid of the dark and why am I paying for it?"

He stopped short when he walked into the living room. Hank was there, all right, but he wasn't alone. And he wasn't unoccupied.

His brother's arms and lips were wrapped around a slip of a female. All Kent could really see of her was a torrent of hair the color of a summer sunset.

"Hank?" This time, there was a note of confusion in Kent's voice.

Breaking away reluctantly, Hank finally responded and looked over at his brother. Eleven months apart, with Kent being the older, they looked more like one another than either looked like Will or Quint.

"Yeah, it's me." He turned the woman around so that she stood with her back to him, facing his brother. Hank tucked his arms around her, more to give her silent support than from the thrill of possession. Pride filled his voice as he ushered the woman forward. "Kent, I'd like you to meet Fiona Reilly." From behind, he kissed her hair. "The woman I'm going to marry."

Kent looked at Hank, too stunned to utter a word. Of all of them, it was Hank who had been the real ladies' man. Hank who'd always had his choice of every unmarried woman under the age of seventy within a fifty-mile radius, and Hank who had to all but beat them back with the proverbial stick.

Hank had always had such a good time being in demand, Kent figured he was never going to become serious enough to settle down. Obviously, he'd figured wrong.

"Does Ma know?"

Looking at the woman in front of Hank more closely, Kent decided that she was a pretty little thing. Far less flashy than the women Kent was accustomed to seeing in Hank's company.

There was an air of subtle class about her. He figured that was good for Hank. But marriage? That was a whole different matter and was going to take some getting used to.

"Not yet." Hank flushed slightly. "I thought we'd stop here first before we tackled breaking the news to her and Dad. Fiona, this is my brother, Kent." His eyes shifted to Kent's companion. Nice, he mused. Very nice. Kent's taste had obviously improved. Who was she? "I would introduce you to the lady with him, but he hasn't told me her name."

Hank looked at his older brother with unabashed curiosity. He rarely saw Kent in the same room with a woman, much less in his own house. She had to be someone special to Kent for that to happen.

Brianne didn't wait for Kent to find his tongue. She stepped forward, her hand out to Hank. "I'm Brianne Gainsborough. My father's a friend of your father's."

"Sure." Hank made the connection immediately. "Brian Gainsborough." He took her hand and was impressed with the heartiness of her handshake. "Dad talks about him all the time."

Kent narrowed his eyes, looking at Hank. Since when? "He does?"

Hank laughed. "You wouldn't know. You never listen to anything that doesn't have the word cattle somewhere in the middle of it." He tucked his arm around Fiona. "Kent runs the Shady Lady for my folks."

She looked a little uneasy, Kent thought, studying the woman his brother had brought into their midst. Thinking about it, he had to admit he felt a little sorry for her. It had to be a scary prospect, meeting your future in-laws for the first time.

"They let me play cowboy," he told her deprecatingly.

Brianne looked at him, surprised at the note of humility in Kent's voice. This was a first.

"Don't let him fool you. Kent works hard at running this ranch," Hank said, his attention focusing on Brianne. Just how did she figure in all this? It didn't take someone with twenty-twenty vision to see that there was some kind of tension going on between them. *Welcome back to the living, brother.* "Are you here for a visit?" he asked Brianne.

She slanted a look at Kent, wondering just how much he was willing to tell his brother. "In a manner of speaking. I'm photographing Kent."

Hank couldn't visualize Kent posing. He did a disappearing act every time their mother tried to take a group photograph at Christmas. "Why and how many lenses have you broken so far?"

Brianne mimicked his tone perfectly as she answered. "For an article in a series on the vanishing cowboy I'm doing and none."

Hank pretended to be amazed. "Must be using more powerful equipment than I thought."

Unwilling to stand around listening to this discussion, Kent walked over to the nearest lamp and turned it off. He roamed the room, turning off other lights. All they needed was one. "Why are all the lights on?"

"Oh, that," Hank had almost forgotten. Being with Fiona tended to make him forget a great many things—except how much he loved her. "I was just showing Fiona around your house, letting her see Will's handiwork firsthand."

"It really is a lovely house, Kent," Fiona said.

Kent shrugged. He never gave or received compliments with any sort of grace or flair. If he'd had his choice, he would just as soon ignore both ends altogether. "It's all right."

"Don't let Will hear you being so careless about his work," Hank warned. "Will's very touchy about his designs," he confided to Fiona, then grinned in Kent's direction. "Kent's just touchy." He winked at Brianne. "But I figure if you've spent more than five minutes with him, you've already figured that out."

"Pretty much," Brianne allowed. She saw the look Kent gave her. What she'd seen earlier in his eyes was gone. So much for their unspoken plans for the rest of the evening. Restless, edgy, she tried to focus her attention on Hank and Fiona. "So, when are you planning to get married?"

Hank pressed a kiss to Fiona's temple. "Soon. Very soon."

If the kiss he'd witnessed when he'd walked in was any indication of the way they felt about each other, Kent figured the wedding should have already taken place—like yesterday.

Kent's usual wariness had quickly faded when confronted with Fiona's manner. He saw what he perceived as genuine love in the woman's eyes whenever she looked at his brother. That was good enough for him.

Funny how he could see things so clearly when it came to other members of his family, yet remained so confused when it came to things that concerned him. Maybe, he thought, that was just the way things were supposed to be.

"Are you going to have the wedding here?" Kent asked Hank. He knew that would make their parents happy, especially his mother. And he had to admit, he had absolutely no interest in going to California. They had nothing there that remotely rivaled anything he could find here.

Hank looked at Fiona for final confirmation before answering. They'd already discussed it, but that was before she'd actually come out here. Maybe the sight of all the trees and endless miles of grass had made her miss home instead.

But Fiona nodded. She could see herself getting married outdoors, beneath a sky so blue it looked as if it had been painted in.

"Seems easier than hog-tying Dad and bringing him down to Southern California," Hank said.

Kent had observed the exchange of looks between his brother and Fiona. He didn't care for it. Did marriage mean that Hank was suddenly on a short leash?

Was that what love did to you? Make you hand over your individuality to someone else?

Maybe he'd been lucky that he and Rosemary had parted company after all.

Kent decided to hold back on his snap judgment regarding Fiona until he got to know her better. Maybe the sweet demeanor that seemed to be her makeup was merely camouflage to throw everyone off.

The way Rosemary's had been.

Brianne detected definite tension between Fiona and Hank, but only when the subject of the wedding arose. "Need moral support?" Brianne guessed.

A light leaped into Fiona's green eyes, followed by a rueful smile. It was silly to feel like this. After all, she was a grown woman. But while she more than held her own running the thriving catering business she had set up, personal one on ones left her terrified.

"Perhaps," Fiona admitted, "just a little."

Brianne had thought as much. "I'm staying at the house for another week. Why don't we all go over there? They should be finished with dinner by now." She looked at Kent significantly.

Hank caught the look and wondered again what was going on between his brother and this very sexy-looking lady. He turned toward Fiona. "What do you say, Fiona? Feel up to it?"

No, she didn't, Fiona thought, an iciness threatening to part her from the light snack she'd had on the road half an hour earlier. But putting the meeting off only made things worse.

So, sternly telling herself she needed to be more self-assured than something evolving out of the rodent family, she nodded. "Sure."

It sounded as if Hank and Fiona hadn't planned on seeing his parents tonight. Kent looked at his brother. "If you weren't going to see them tonight, just where were you figuring on staying the night?"

"Here." The answer seemed rather obvious to Hank. Will had given the place three bedrooms, although why, when it was for Kent, Hank had no idea. "You've got more than enough room."

And then his glance darted toward Brianne, who was even now chatting with Fiona about the architecture of the house, doing her damnedest to put the other young woman at her ease. Hank took an instant liking to her. Looked to him as if Kent had finally gotten lucky, whether he realized it or not.

Turning so that Brianne couldn't see him, Hank grinned broadly at Kent. "Unless, of course, we would be interrupting something."

There were times when guarding his space meant keeping out members of his family as well. Right now, Kent hadn't a clue as to what he was really doing in this situation, so letting others in on it was out of the question. He wasn't about to share his feelings with Hank. From the lovestruck look in his younger brother's eyes, all he'd get would be meaningless platitudes about love conquering all and nonsense like that.

Not that the word love even entered into the situation. Trouble was, he wasn't sure just what word did enter into it.

"No, you wouldn't be interrupting anything," Kent assured him. "She just wanted to look around, same as Fiona. For her article," he added, as an afterthought. He hoped that Hank wouldn't notice Brianne had no camera with her.

Though she was talking to Fiona, Brianne heard what Kent said to his brother. The sting of irritating disappointment was sharp enough that it almost made her wince. Was he ashamed to admit to his brother that they were going to spend the night together, or just embarrassed?

Or was it that she had somehow misread the signals he was giving off?

No, she was sure she hadn't. The signals weren't a mystery.

Only the man was.

She refused to let him see that his complete reversal bothered her in the slightest. If he could shrug her off so easily, she could do the same with him.

Brianne looked at Fiona. She might as well make herself useful.

"Don't worry," she assured the other woman. "Mr. and Mrs. Cutler are very nice people." She slanted a glance at Kent. "They're so warm, it's hard to believe that they had a son like Kent."

His expression was dark as he ushered her out the door behind his brother and Fiona. "About before."

"Before?" Brianne looked at him innocently.

There was no way she was going to let him see that she was hurt. That she'd wanted him more than she'd thought ever possible. That she still wanted him. That was her problem to deal with, not his. "Was there a before?"

Kent pressed his lips together. Maybe this was the way to go. Best to pretend that nothing had gone on between them, that nothing would have gone on between them had the house been empty.

Yeah, right.

But the opportunity to spend the night was gone and maybe that, too, was for the best. You can't miss what you never had. And she would be, after all, on the East Coast within the week.

He nodded, closing the door behind him. "As long as we understand each other."

Brianne merely shook her head. "Oh, I understand you, Kent Cutler," she said, softly enough for only him to hear. "You're scared." Scared of feeling, scared of letting yourself go, she thought.

Sarcasm twisted his lips into a smile that failed to reach his eyes. "Right. I'm scared of you. You scare the hell out of me."

Now that, Brianne thought, was just her point. One that was going to have to strike home before he could ever allow himself to feel anything. "Truer words were never spoken."

He figured it was safer not to comment on that. Instead, he turned toward his brother. "Mind if she rides with you?"

Hank looked surprised at the request. He wondered

if Kent was doing his usual backing-away trick. If he was, he was an idiot.

"Fine with me." Hank opened the rear passenger door for Brianne.

Smiling her thanks, Brianne very deliberately closed the door again, "I wouldn't dream of imposing. You two deserve to be alone. I'll go back the way I came." She looked at Kent, daring him to tell her she couldn't. "On Whiskey."

"You let her ride your horse?" Hank asked, amazed. As far as he knew, Kent never let anyone near the quarter horse.

"Only when he's on it," Brianne answered.

Kent scowled. "I can talk for myself," Kent told her. Why was she always pushing her way into things?

"Not nearly fast enough." She waited expectantly as he mounted.

Reluctantly, because his brother and Fiona were watching, Kent extended his hand to Brianne. "If you mean that I don't talk as fast as you do, hell, lady, the wind doesn't move as fast as your mouth does."

Hank laughed as he started his car. "I think those two have got the makings of a great couple."

"Someone should tell your brother," Fiona suggested.

"Oh, he knows, Fiona." Hank smiled to himself. *And about time, too.* "He knows."

For a woman who was accustomed to the hard life on the range, who had gone through some really rough economic times, during both her childhood and her marriage, his mother cried far too much, Kent thought. She cried whenever they looked at the family album. She cried when she listened to sad music, or watched something sad on television. Once he'd even caught her crying softly while listening to an old tape of them singing Christmas carols when they were kids. That was when he knew she'd never change.

So it came as no surprise to him when she began to cry as soon as Hank had introduced her to Fiona and told them that they were getting married.

Zoe's eyes sparkled like the diamonds she'd never asked for. Her heart felt as if it was bursting as she looked at her future daughter-in-law. The family needed more women in it. "A wedding. How wonderful."

Chasing away all of Fiona's unspoken fears, she opened her arms wide.

"Welcome to the family, Fiona."

Relieved, Fiona hugged the older woman. Jake added his arms to the tangle, as did Hank. Unwilling to join this human knot, Kent kept his distance and muttered under his breath. These public displays of affection weren't for him.

Brianne watched the same expression of emotion and felt, just for a second, a touch of envy. She expected it to be gone the next moment.

But it wasn't.

It just reminded her of something that she'd never had. Something, she assumed, that she probably wasn't destined to have in the near foreseeable future.

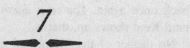

7

"He'll be here."

Turning at the sound of the voice behind her, Brianne raised her eyes innocently to Will, looking at him over the rim of her glass. The oldest of the Cutler siblings was blonder and more soft-spoken than his brothers. Having gone through two rolls of film already, she'd decided to take a break.

Her expression indicated that she hadn't the faintest clue whom he was talking about. As if she hadn't kept one eye on the back door the entire time, watching as half the town arrived at the party his parents were holding in what was whimsically referred to as their backyard. "Whimsically," because to the naked eye it appeared endless.

"Who?"

It had been a long time since Will had been taken in by a pretty woman and Will wasn't taken in now. Brianne knew exactly whom he was talking about. He'd seen the way she was eyeing the door.

"That backward little brother of mine." A few feet away, the band that Quint had helped put together for the impromptu party was playing one of the many toe-tapping tunes in its repertoire. Will retired the almost empty glass he was holding to the nearest surface he could find and looked at Brianne. "Dance with me?" He saw her eyes dart toward the back once again. *You're a damn fool, Kent.* "Just until Kent shows up, that is."

No danger of that. Kent had mumbled some excuse when his mother had announced she was throwing together this party for Hank and Fiona. It had taken the combined efforts of the Cutlers, including Kent, to pull it off in less than twenty-four hours. But when it came to attending, Kent had drawn the line.

"In that case, you might be forced to dance with me all night," Brianne warned him, setting her own glass down beside his.

His smile was warm and inviting. Why couldn't Kent look at her like that, she wondered in silent annoyance. Why couldn't he be more like his brothers? And why did she have to be attracted to a surly scowl and a kiss that tasted like secret sin?

"I can think of worse fates." Waiting, Will held his hands out to her.

Brianne could feel the effects of the punch she'd just downed. It had, thanks to Jake, a very real kick to it. The kind that took you by surprise.

A little like Kent's kiss, she thought sadly.

No, no sad thoughts tonight. There was a party going on and she thoroughly intended to enjoy herself, even if that stubborn bastard didn't show up.

With a toss of her head that sent her blond hair

flying over her shoulder, she took Will up on his invitation. ''I'd love to dance with you, Will.''

Taking her hand, Will led Brianne over to the lantern-lined area that had been set aside for dancing just as the band began another, even livelier set.

It looked to him as if everyone his parents had invited to this impromptu celebration of Hank and Fiona's engagement had shown up and brought a friend along with them. The area behind the house was teeming with people. Voices raised in conversation or laughter mixed with the rhythmic music of the guitars and drums.

As he took her into his arms, Will let his eyes skim along the dress Brianne had on. Hugging all her curves, it made a man's mouth water. Her long, straight hair poured over her shoulders like a golden shower and gleamed in the lantern light. Kent had no idea what he was missing.

''Don't misunderstand,'' Will began, trying his best to make a case for his irrational brother and excuse his behavior, ''I love Kent—''

''Like a brother,'' she teased with a grin.

''Yeah—'' He laughed. ''At times.'' Other times, like now, he was tempted to do a number on Kent's numbskull. ''But I'll admit he can be very pigheaded and set in his ways.''

''Tell me something I don't already know.'' She'd had two glasses of punch before Will had found her, and maybe because it had chased away any inhibitions she might have still held, Brianne found herself wanting to confide in Will. She needed an honest

opinion. Leaning into him even though the song that
was being played was not a slow ballad, but a fast
number, she whispered against his ear, "Will, can I
ask you a question?"

Lord, how could Kent find it in himself to resist
this woman? "Shoot."

"Is there anything wrong with me?"

Will frowned, drawing his head back so he could
look at her. "What do you mean?"

Wasn't she speaking clearly? Brianne forced herself to focus and hang on to her spinning head. "Just
that. Is there anything wrong with me? Something
that might make someone keep away from me."

The question was so ridiculous, Will could only
laugh. "Lady, if there was anything more right, it'd
be illegal for you to go outdoors."

"Then why is Kent—?"

He spared her the embarrassment of going on.
"Not here?"

She sighed, then rested her cheek against his
shoulder. "Among other things."

Very fraternal feelings nudged at Will. For
Brianne, not his brother. There was no reason for
Kent to make her feel so bad. He debated having
Kent horsewhipped. "Because he's afraid."

That's what she had said to Kent last night, but
Brianne was beginning to have her doubts that she'd
been right. Maybe it had just been overconfidence
doing the talking. Kent's no-show had certainly shot
her overconfidence to smithereens.

"Your brother doesn't strike me as the kind of man who's afraid."

Will thought that over carefully. "Not of much," he agreed. "But when it comes to matters close to the heart, I think he might be spooked."

That didn't bear out, either. "But he kissed me," she protested.

Will chuckled as he turned around on the floor with her. "More than once, so I hear." He grinned when she didn't raise her head to look at him, or offer a protest. "You're not surprised I know."

She lifted a shoulder in a half shrug. "People talk in small towns. Everyone except for Kent," she amended. "Kent doesn't do anything the way he should." The punch wasn't through with her yet as she felt another wave of emotion spike. "If he's so damn self-contained, why *did* he kiss me?"

"Because he isn't so self-contained as he wants everyone to think he is. Because there's something going on between the two of you that he can't control." Will guided her between two couples, out of the way of a collision in the making. "Maybe that scares him, too," he considered. He saw her eyebrows rise in a silent question. "The fact that he's attracted to you even though he doesn't want to be."

"Why can't he just simply enjoy the attraction and let it go at that?"

She'd known so many men like that, men who lived for the moment and gave no thought to tomorrow. She'd never thought of that as a particularly commendable quality, until just now. She wanted

Kent to loosen up, to enjoy the time they had left rather than turn it into a silent war of wills.

Will shrugged. "Kent's an all-or-nothing kind of guy." He tried to make her understand. "When he took over running the Shady Lady, the ranch had fallen on hard times again." As the oldest, he remembered both extremes all too well. The peaks and the valleys. "We've had our up-and-down periods on the ranch because of the economy and such." He wasn't going to bore her with details about cattle prices and winters so cold they destroyed everything in their path. It was enough just to mention the outcome. "But Kent took it personally. He researched the problem, read all the latest books on ranching—"

"Kent?" She couldn't picture the man who had moved so quickly through his chores each day having the patience to crack a book, no matter what the reason. A whip, certainly, but not a book.

"Kent." Will knew what she was thinking. There was a deeper side to Kent that only the family was privy to. "Don't let that hooded-eye cowboy exterior fool you. He's got a bachelor's degree from the university." Kent could be damn dedicated and hard-nosed about it when he wanted to be. "While the rest of us went off to try our wings in other directions, Kent devoted himself completely to putting the ranch in the black again—with a vengeance."

Will nodded a greeting at someone behind her. Over to one side, people were line-dancing, but he preferred facing her and holding her in his arms.

"There's a tradition behind the Shady Lady. The

ranch has been in the family for over two hundred years and Kent means to get it thriving. Pretty much succeeded, as I see it." He knew his parents would have sold the Shady Lady at one point, if it hadn't been for Kent. That was right after his father had had his heart attack and the price of beef fell. Selling would have been a gross mistake. "You've got to give him a little more time."

Maybe, if things were different. But that wasn't a viable option for her. "Time is what I don't have. I'm leaving at the end of the week."

Five days, she thought, five short days. To Kent, they probably seemed endless.

Will studied her. "If he asked you to stay, would you?"

"No." There wasn't just herself to consider. She was a professional and there were people counting on her. "But I'd come back."

"Then come back for the wedding," Hank told her as he cut in. He'd approached them just in time to hear the tail end of the conversation. With a smile, he edged his older brother out of the way and took Brianne into his arms. "Mind if I cut in?" he asked Will after the fact.

Will pretended to look annoyed, but he knew that Hank was just as curious as he was to talk with this woman who had turned Kent on his ear.

Brianne's eyes shifted toward Hank. When he'd first taken her hand, she'd thought for a second that he was Kent. Silly to react this way, she admonished herself, but her heart was playing a drum solo.

"He's supposed to keep dancing with me until Kent comes," she told Hank.

"That's all right, I'll take over." Turning Brianne, he faced his brother. "I'm the best dancer in the family anyway."

"Says who?" Will wanted to know as Hank danced Brianne away.

"Everyone," Hank called back. He turned his attention to Brianne. The one or two times he'd looked her way, she'd seemed preoccupied. "So, is Kent giving you a hard time?"

That was putting it mildly, but what was the use of complaining? This was, after all, his brother. "He's being Kent," she answered vaguely.

Hank didn't need a better explanation than that. "He's giving you a hard time, all right." That was Kent, by definition. "I didn't get a chance to ask before, but what have you done to him?"

The question caught her completely off guard. She blinked, wondering if Hank was pulling her leg, or if he'd had too much of the punch. Like she'd had.

"Excuse me?"

Hank grinned. "We speak our minds out here. Our hearts take a little longer." And that was a shame, but it was the way things were in a land that tended to show little mercy. "Being away for a while, I can see the difference in him." He'd noticed it immediately. Noticed, too, the source of it. And, because he was in love himself, could guess at the reason. "Kent looks like a calf that's being led to the slaughter and is trying his damnedest to resist."

The comparison made her shiver. "That makes me out to be a butcher. Not a very flattering image."

There'd been cattle and cattlemen around him for as far back as he could remember. Hank forgot at times that not everyone was accustomed to the facts of ranching life.

"Sorry, comes with the territory. Seriously, I don't remember ever seeing Kent behave like this." The music stopped, then began again, as a new tune filled the air. "I think it's safe to say that he's got it bad for you."

"No, you've got that wrong. He has it *in* for me because I invaded his sacred space," she corrected. "He really resents the fact that I'm following him around, taking photographs, asking questions."

Hank knew better than anyone that no one could force his brother to do anything. Steel was less set in its way than Kent once he'd made up his mind about something,.

"That's just his act. If Kent doesn't want to do something, he won't. It's as simple as that. No ifs, ands or buts. Kent's not the type to be forced to do anything against his will. Take it from me, I've tried."

Maybe it was the punch, but suddenly it was very important to her that Hank was right. "So if he kissed me—"

"He damn well wanted to, no matter how much he fought against it." Seeing the questioning look in her eyes, Hank hurried to explain. "Oh, the fight has nothing to do with you, it has to do with him. Kent doesn't want to get involved with a woman.''

Brianne looked at Hank curiously. Quint had alluded to some failed romance in Kent's past when she'd first met him, but she'd thought it was just talk. ''Is this some bachelor thing, some pact he made with himself years ago?''

''No, it's not.'' The answer came from behind her. The next moment, Quint was cutting in on his younger brother. ''You've had her long enough, 'Henry.''' He grinned, knowing how much Hank hated being called by his given name. ''It's my turn. You go keep your fiancée company before she comes to her senses and runs off with the first decent man she sees.''

Hank drew his hands from Brianne. ''Then I'd better get to her before Dad does.'' He inclined his head toward Brianne before leaving her with Quint. ''Brianne, it's been a pleasure.''

''Likewise.'' Fiona, she thought, was one lucky lady. As were all the women who would eventually number themselves among the Cutler brides.

Except for Kent's, of course, she added. The woman who got him got a prickly pear. If he ever let a woman close enough for that to happen.

''Kent didn't make a pact with himself, exactly.'' Never skipping a beat, Quint picked up the thread of the conversation he'd interrupted. ''He just plain swore off women, after Rosemary.''

She knew Kent would never tell her anything about himself, least of all about a woman who'd been in his life. Brianne jumped at the opportunity to find out about the mysterious Rosemary when Quint presented it to her.

"Just who *is* Rosemary?"

"Rosemary Taylor." Tucking her hand inside his, Quint pressed it to his shoulder. Dancing with Brianne, he thought, was like dancing on air. Kent was a lucky son of a gun, if only he'd realize it. "Kent had a crush on her all through school."

Try as he might, Quint had never been able to understand what Kent saw in the girl. She was too thin and sharp-featured for his taste. But then, he'd been in the minority.

"They went together when they were in high school." He quoted what others had said about Rosemary, rather than his own assessment. "She had to be the prettiest girl around here. Trouble was, Rosemary didn't want to be around here. She wanted to go off to Hollywood and get a movie career. Kent wanted to stay here. It's where his heart was." The set of Quint's jaw hardened just a little, though his smile remained. "So she ripped it out of him. Rosemary turned down his proposal, left town without him and Kent swore off women permanently. Said they were a puzzle that wasn't worth the trouble of his trying to put together. End of story." He looked at Brianne pointedly. "Until now."

If she'd meant the slightest thing to Kent, even in the way of a casual flirtation, he would have been here by now. The party had begun almost two hours ago. Will, Hank and now Quint were just trying to be nice.

"I think he's just feeling restless, that's all."

Quint knew better. "And whose fault is that?" he pointed out. "He wouldn't be feeling restless if he wasn't feeling something."

The punch had taken the edge off her patience. She didn't want explanations, she wanted Kent. "Then why isn't he here?"

"He'll be here," she heard Jake tell her.

Moving between them, the older man looked at his son expectantly. Quint released Brianne with an accommodating smile.

"I know my sons," Jake told her. Seeing them all take turns dancing with Brianne, he'd decided to try his own hand at it. "Zoe thinks she's got a lock on that." He winked knowingly at Brianne. "But she doesn't. I understand them because, one time or another, I felt like they did about things."

He knew she didn't want to hear an old man recount memories, no matter how polite she was. Jake got down to the part she'd be interested in.

"Kent was always the most stubborn. Even more than Morgan. Too bad she couldn't have been here tonight." He digressed for a moment, wishing that his family could be all together, the way they once had been. Back then, he'd been too busy to enjoy it. Now he knew it was an occasion to savor and celebrate. "They say a man's most partial to his daughter, but it's not true. I think I'm partial to all of them, one way or another." He thought of his middle child.

Middle children were supposed to be easygoing. Kent went against all the rules. "Kent's like a tough piece of meat. You've got to tenderize it some before it releases its flavor."

She liked his simile, but there was a problem with it. "Tenderizing takes time." She told him what she'd told Will. "I don't have any."

Her deadline. Jake remembered Brian saying something about that when he'd called to make the initial arrangements for his daughter. "Can't you get an extension? Stay a while longer?" He knew Kent couldn't hold out forever. If he tried to, there were his brothers around to beat some sense into his thick head.

Brianne shook her head. "No, my editor was very firm. Besides, Kent made it clear that I've overstayed my welcome—from the first day." And a woman could only make herself so available before it became pathetic.

"Don't you believe it. That's just his way. If he wasn't acting like that tough cowboy you see, he wouldn't know how to behave. He doesn't quite believe that it's all right to let your guard down. Kent's still trying to figure it all out."

A lot of good that'd do her after this week. "By then, we all might be dead," she quipped.

Jake laughed. He liked this one. The girl had spunk, something that always came in handy around these parts. Maybe he'd see about giving Kent a well-placed nudge. "He's slow, but he's not that slow."

* * *

Enough was enough.

His eyes on Brianne, Kent cut through the crowd between him and his goal. He'd arrived quietly some time ago, and had been looking on long enough to see every man in his family take a turn on the floor with Brianne. He'd watched them dance and talk.

What was she doing, pumping each of them for information? He wouldn't doubt it. The woman just couldn't seem to leave his life alone.

Just like she couldn't leave his mind alone.

Well, at least he could put a stop to her asking questions. He made his way over to where his father was dancing with Brianne.

If you could call it dancing, he thought. His father's idea of dancing was standing in one place and lifting his feet up and down while someone played music.

"Dad, Ma's looking for you," Kent said to him, purposely ignoring Brianne.

He had no idea what had made him say that to his father, only that he didn't want Brianne dancing with anyone else, even Jake Cutler. Didn't want her dancing with anyone else, didn't want her laughing with anyone else in that way of hers, or even placing her hand on their arm. Most of all, he didn't want her head resting on their chest with the sweet scent that was trapped in her hair wafting up to them. Stirring them the way it stirred him.

Jake looked at Kent knowingly. He'd seen him arrive earlier and hang back. *Took you damn long enough,* he thought.

"Well, then I'd better let her find me." Taking Brianne's hand, he placed it in Kent's. "Here, take over for me. Dance with the lady," Jake urged as he walked away.

Brianne dropped her hand. She didn't need anyone begging Kent on her behalf. If he'd wanted to dance with her, he would have cut in, like all the others. "That's all right, I'm all danced out."

Kent caught her hand again before she had a chance to get away. Brianne tugged once, but he just tightened his hold. She looked at him questioningly.

"What is it, you dance with all the men in my family but me?" he demanded.

She stared at him. She thought he'd just gotten here. Apparently not. "How did you know I danced with them?"

He drew her into his arms as the music began again. She fit easily, as if she belonged there. He didn't want to think about that. "That's a fool question. How would I know? I saw you."

"You were watching?" Just how long had Kent been here?

As the tempo of the song increased, his movements became quicker. It pleased Kent that she was keeping up without seeming to realize it. "It's not against the law, as far as I know."

It might not be illegal, but it was rude. "Why didn't you come over?"

He spread one hand wide before he wrapped it around her again. "I did." He spun her around twice, then pulled her to him once more.

Face-to-face, she glared at him. He knew what she meant. "Sooner."

Hands on his belt, he did a little heel-and-toe step, then watched as she mimicked it. The woman had promise. "I didn't want to."

Getting into the spirit of the competition, she did her best to keep up. "And now?"

He took hold of her again, dancing with her instead of beside her. In every sense of the word, she was a handful. "Woman, you ask too many damn questions."

Brianne lifted her chin pugnaciously. "That's because you don't give me any answers."

How could she say that? "What the hell was all that before?"

She grinned. "Fancy footwork."

Did she think she was going to get off with a smart remark? "You want to see fancy footwork? Hang on, lady. You ain't seen nothing yet."

He was right, Brianne hadn't.

By the time the song finally faded away, they'd managed to clear a small space around them as others dropped out, content to watch the show rather than compete with it. She was aware of a flash going off at one point, and saw Will retreat, grinning and holding an old instant camera in his hands.

She supposed it was only fair. She'd been snapping photographs of the people at the party all evening, a sort of busman's holiday. She made a mental note to ask Will to see the photograph he'd taken.

Breathless, she gladly followed Kent from the

dance area when he finally retreated. "Kent, you really surprised me. I didn't know you had it in you."

He looked at her over his shoulder. "Lot of things you don't know about me."

"Teach me."

The softly voiced words felt like a thunderclap as Kent absorbed them. He debated, wavered, then finally shrugged.

Brianne had no idea if he was shrugging away his shell, or her entreaty.

"Want some punch?" She was just recovering from the effects of what she'd already consumed, but she nodded anyway. "C'mon, then, let's go get some and go somewhere more private. There's way too many people around here to suit me."

Brianne looked around. Leaving didn't seem polite. "Won't your mother mind?"

"Mind? She won't even miss me." He poured a glass, then handed it to her. "You, maybe. She'd notice you were gone under normal circumstances. But right now, her attention is on her baby boy and his fiancée."

The remark was said without malice. Affection for the members of his family wasn't something he talked about, but he felt it just the same.

With the glass he'd poured for himself in one hand, he put out the other to her. "Coming?"

Ready for anything, Brianne placed her hand in his. "Coming."

A small thrill shivered through her as he closed his fingers over hers.

8

She wasn't sure just where Kent was taking her. Hands linked, they walked away from the house until the sound of the party in the back was a dull buzz instead of a loud roar.

It never ceased to amaze Brianne how dark it was out here, with only the moon to light the way. She'd been a city girl too long, she mused.

How far were they going? She knew they weren't going to walk to his house and there was nothing in between. They'd gone in the opposite direction from the barn. What was left?

Just as she was going to ask, Kent stopped walking. Obviously, they'd arrived.

Brianne looked around. Maybe there was hope for him yet. For someone who tried so hard to be stoic, he'd picked a very romantic spot. It was a grassy hill that overlooked the winding Yellowstone River far below. From here, it looked like a wide, velvet ribbon with flecks of silver on it where the moon had scattered its beams on the water.

Kent had chosen this spot for a reason. He'd carved his initials on one of the trees here long ago.

His and Rosemary's. In case he forgot what letting a woman get under your skin ultimately accomplished, the tree would serve as a silent reminder.

If only he remembered to look at it.

Brianne turned from the view to look at Kent. He hadn't said two words since they'd slipped away. Maybe he felt that the land could do his talking for him. But she wanted to hear his voice, even if it wasn't as eloquent as the scenery around them.

Looking for something to say that wouldn't fuel another disagreement between them, she commented on his brother. "Hank looks happy."

Kent smiled to himself. He'd wondered how long it would take before she finally broke down and said something. She'd lasted longer than he'd thought. If it were up to him, he could probably have prolonged the silence indefinitely. But Brianne seemed to need to fill the space up with words. All manner of words. It was an annoying habit, but it was growing progressively less so. Or maybe he was just getting more tolerant.

"Yeah, he does, doesn't he?" He paused to slowly sip the glass of punch he'd brought with him. His father must have put in a double dose of his "special additive" in honor of the occasion, Kent mused, the half smile growing larger. "But then, it never took much with Hank." Kent raised a silent toast to his brother and his good fortune. He sincerely hoped Hank would be luckier at love than he'd been. "He always had a happy disposition."

She couldn't quite make out if Kent was sneering

at that or not. "You say that like it's a foreign state of being."

He shrugged, drinking a little more. Too bad he hadn't thought to bring a flask with him. There were times when a man just wanted to sit in the darkness, toast the past and tie one on slowly.

The flask wouldn't have done any good, he decided. Having Brianne with him centered his thoughts on the present rather than the past and negated any chance of getting a pleasant buzz.

That, he reminded himself, was his own doing.

"For some of us it is," Kent admitted. It was a long time since he could remember being really happy. "For some of us, the best we can shoot for is being content." He considered that. "Or maybe just the absence of discord."

For a minute, he'd almost taken her in. But to shoot for only the absence of discord lacked passion. Try as he might to pretend otherwise, Kent did not lack passion. She'd witnessed it, sampled it. She'd tasted it on his lips when he'd kissed her.

Turning, Brianne found herself almost against him. She didn't step back. "Oh, I think you can shoot for more than that."

The hot evening breeze was playing with the scent she wore, swirling it around his head so that Kent felt just a shade dizzy from it. It still didn't dull his mind. But it clouded it a little.

"Maybe I could, but I won't." He moved to straighten, then thought better of it. Maybe, just this once, he'd enjoy the lady. He figured it was the punch talking. At least it was easier to blame what he was feeling on that than his own weakening resistance. "Don't have the time. The ranch takes it all up."

He was hiding behind that excuse and they both knew it. This Rosemary person she'd been told about had definitely burnt him. But all scars healed eventually if you didn't pick at them and Kent didn't strike her as someone who'd pull at a scab.

Brianne smiled at him. "I don't see the ranch taking up your time right now."

No, but she was, he thought. She took up his time and his mind and even if it would soon be over, he shouldn't be allowing this obstruction to be occurring at all. The tug-of-war in his mind between logic and needs seemed doomed to continue. "Takes more than a stray hour here and there to make a relationship."

She was surprised that they agreed on something. It took a great deal of work to maintain a relationship. But it all began with that first step. "True, but it's a start."

He wasn't about to start a relationship. A relationship that had nowhere to go. He downed the rest of his drink, then dropped the glass on the grass near his feet. He looked at the river, avoiding her eyes. "Maybe, maybe not."

He was dancing around more now than he had on the floor with her. The chance agreement, she supposed, was a fluke. "Did you bring me out here to argue?"

His eyes shifted toward her. To her face. Moonlight was kind to her, he thought, caressing her limbs, her skin. Making her look like something out of a dream. Maybe even his dream. He touched her hair. "No, I didn't have arguing in mind."

His eyes held her fast. "What did you have in mind?"

He didn't answer immediately. Instead, he took her into his arms. "I think you know."

She threaded her arms under his, content to remain here like this with him for a very long time. "Tell me."

Why did she always want to talk? "I'm a man of few words."

Brianne snapped her fingers as if she'd forgotten that. As if that were possible.

"That's right." Her eyes were laughing at him. "Then show me," she coaxed, her words a soft whisper.

He'd like to show her. Show her all night long. Slowly, patiently.

Who was he kidding? The first time they came together it would be like two volcanoes going off, all noise and fire.

He didn't know how much longer he could hold himself back. He wasn't even clear as to why any longer.

Kent shook his head. "You know nothing's going to come of this."

"Didn't ask it to," she reminded him. She wanted

him to know that strings weren't part of the deal. ''Whatever happens, happens.''

She believed that, he thought, taking her at her word. ''Good enough.''

Surprising her, he gently touched his mouth to hers, then deepened the kiss by small degrees.

It didn't matter how it happened, the results were always the same, Brianne thought. He'd heightened all her senses so that she was acutely aware of everything around her.

She was aware of the noise in the background, the sound of crickets close by. She was aware of the pounding of her own heart. Most of all, she was aware of the touch, taste and scent of the man who was swiftly on his way to becoming a habit.

A habit she was finding that she didn't want to break.

Kent drew back, framing her face in his hands as he searched it for something he wasn't all that certain he wanted to see. There were twin images of him reflected in her eyes. Shimmering. Trapped. Was that how it was? Was his soul trapped within hers now? Was it just that simple?

He sighed. ''Woman, how do you get your lips to taste like that?''

Brianne was only just now coming around. His kiss seemed to devastate her the way nothing else could. She blinked, trying to make sense of his question.

She wasn't aware that her lips had any taste to

them at all. She barely remembered wearing lipstick.
"Like what?"

"Bottled sin." If sin could be bottled and sampled,
Kent knew that it would taste exactly that way. Exactly like Brianne's lips.

Had it been raining, the smile in her eyes would
have instantly dried him with its heat. "Trade secret."

"You're entitled," he murmured, taking another
sample. With his hand beneath her chin, he tilted her
head back and lost himself within her. God, but a
man could get hooked on this. Hooked bad.

"I had a feeling you might be here. We're going
to have a toast now, or are you two having your own
private party?"

Kent's head jerked up to see Quint coming toward
them, the grin on his face wide enough to drive a
truck through. Damn it, this country just wasn't big
enough anymore. "You policing the party, now?"

Quint'd had a hunch that Kent might come by
here. As far as he knew, he was the only one Kent
had told about the initials carved on the side of the
tree facing the lake. Not even Rosemary knew. Kent
never got the chance to tell her.

Quint laughed at the moodily posed question. "If
I were, you two would be run in for setting a fire
without the proper ordinances." He allowed himself
one glance at Brianne's flushed face before training
his gaze on Kent. "Ma sent me looking for you
two."

Brianne collected herself quickly and now triumph

lighted her features as she slanted a glance at Kent. "See, I told you she'd miss us."

"Actually, she sent me looking for you," he confessed to Brianne. Quint flashed Kent an apologetic look. "Ma still doesn't know you're here."

There was a reason for that. Kent hadn't sought his mother out when he arrived. He'd thought to slip in quietly and just observe the party from the sidelines. He wound up observing Brianne instead.

Kent eyed the faded initials he'd carved. Maybe it was time to fell this tree, he mused. Or carve something over the initials.

"Maybe we should keep it that way," he suggested. "Take Brianne with you, I'll go home."

Quint shook his head. "C'mon, I found you, I'm bound to bring you back." Quint took Kent's arm to give him a little shove in the right direction.

Kent drew his arm away. "You know how I feel about crowds like this."

"It'll be painless, I promise. Humor Mom. She likes this kind of stuff."

"Just because she likes it, why do I have to suffer through it?" Kent sighed, surrendering. Without thinking, he tucked his arm around Brianne's waist. "Well, it could be worse. I could be the one getting married."

"Ha, nobody'd ever have you." Quint laughed. "Right, Brianne?"

"Nobody I know," she agreed.

Kent scowled. Why did the right answer sound so

wrong, coming from her? "We might as well get this over with."

Quint looked around Kent's shoulders at Brianne. "He loves to put up a fuss, but he just wants to be coerced. He doesn't mind family get-togethers nearly as much as he claims to."

"You could have fooled me," Brianne commented, looking at Kent's face.

That, Kent thought, was the main idea.

He wasn't ready for daylight.

Muttering an oath, Kent dragged himself into a sitting position, swinging his legs over the side of the bed. He remained there for several minutes, trying to get his bearings.

Slowly, awareness of his surroundings penetrated the fog that always encircled his brain first thing in the morning. He realized with a start that Brianne had gotten up ahead of him and was already here.

He could smell the evidence.

Though he hated to admit it, he was getting accustomed to waking up to the scent of fresh-brewed coffee and pancakes sizzling on the grill.

Kent rubbed his hands over his face. He couldn't believe she was here. No matter how early he'd awakened this past week, she always managed to be up sooner. She'd been here every morning, in his kitchen, as if making breakfast was somehow a silent part of the bargain even when he told her it wasn't.

Because the party had gone on until the wee hours

of Monday morning, Kent was certain that there was no way Brianne would be here so early.

If he'd placed a bet on it, he would have lost.

The woman took a perverse pleasure in being annoying. Rubbing the last bit of sleep from his eyes, Kent got dressed as quickly as he could. He wanted no repeat performances of that first morning when she'd seen him in the altogether.

At least, not unless Brianne was wearing the same thing.

His thoughts were turning that way more and more, Kent realized. He supposed he should be grateful that she was leaving in five days. The fact that he wasn't just told him that there was something going seriously wrong with him.

He didn't want to be accustomed to the sight of her, didn't want to subconsciously feel that if he ventured out to his kitchen, no matter how early the hour, she'd be there, doing things to make his mouth water.

Some of it even having to do with food.

No, this wasn't good at all.

"Why aren't you in bed?" Kent asked accusingly as he walked into the kitchen.

Brianne was getting used to his surly greetings each morning. Jake's remark, that if Kent wasn't playing the part of an ornery cowboy he wouldn't know how to behave, came back to her. Brianne decided that Kent's father could very well have something there.

She smiled as she turned to look at him, a plate

of hot pancakes fresh off the grill in her hands. ''Is that an invitation?''

He lowered himself into his chair. The memory of last night insisted on lodging itself in the center of his thoughts. Who knew where the kiss would have led if Quint hadn't come poking around? If things had gone their natural way, maybe he wouldn't feel like a wounded bear that had been deprived.

''You are the most brazen woman I've ever met.''

''That's because you only socialize with cattle.'' She placed the plate in front of him, then reached for the coffeepot. ''And, to answer your question, for your information, I haven't been to bed yet.''

He raised a brow in surprise. ''Why not?''

Contrary to his intention, Kent had remained at the party until it had broken up and all of the guests had left. That was at 1:30. What had she been doing between then and now?

And with whom?

There it was again, he thought crossly, that possessive feeling he not only had no right to, but no desire to lay claim to. If he didn't know better, he'd say that the woman was turning him inside out for her own amusement.

''I helped your mother and Fiona clean up, and then I had something to do.''

Taking the mug in his hands, he drank the first swallow quickly, letting the hot liquid course through his veins and bring him back among the living.

Setting it down, he waited, but she didn't continue.

"Are you going to tell me, or are you going to make me ask you?"

She took one pancake for herself, then picked up the coffee she'd been sipping and came over to join him. "Nice to know you have some curiosity. I was beginning to think you weren't human."

If he wasn't human, he wouldn't be aching for her like this. He waved a hand at her, dismissing her words, losing whatever shreds of patience he had left.

"All right, don't tell me. Makes no difference to me. I was just trying to be sociable."

She laughed as she sat down opposite him. "That'll be the day." There was no secret to what she had been doing. She was more than happy to share it with him. "I stayed up developing the photographs I took at the party."

"What's the hurry?" She hadn't yet developed any of the photographs she'd taken earlier in the week. He knew her. If she'd developed them, she would have buttonholed him and shown the photographs to him.

He knew her.

The phrase played along his brain, taunting him. Numbing him with its implication. He didn't want to know her. He wanted to remain strangers. You never thought about strangers once they left.

Brianne wondered what was behind Kent's strange expression, but said nothing. She wasn't in the mood for a sparring match first thing in the morning. She was much too tired today.

"I thought it might make a nice present for Hank

and Fiona," she explained. "A souvenir of their first party together."

"You did that for them?" The thoughtfulness surprised him. "Why?"

There he went again, sounding suspicious. "Because they're nice people. And I'm nice people. And that's what nice people do."

She blew out a breath, holding her mug between her hands. Her head ached from too much punch and her body ached from lack of sleep. Even more, it ached from lack of loving. His loving. No man had ever affected her this way before. He provoked her and made her happy all at the same time. Most of all, he confused her. She felt her nerves pulling taut.

"Why are you always so suspicious of everything?" she demanded. She was tired of having everything she said pulled apart and examined for a hidden agenda, a covert meaning.

The edginess in her voice surprised him. She usually faced his questions with amusement. "Not everything."

"Just me." It was the only logical conclusion.

His eyes met hers as he drank the last of the coffee. He was going to need a second cup if he was going to get through the morning with her. "Just you."

"Why?"

Kent took his time answering. He poured himself a second mugful. "I thought you didn't like that question."

He was deliberately trying to provoke her. The

headache grew more intense. "Only when it's aimed at me like the barrel of a Colt .45."

"Nobody uses those anymore," he informed her carelessly, enjoying himself. She didn't usually get rattled. Nice to see her true colors.

Brianne didn't care if people around here shot cannons at each other. He was deliberately being evasive. "Don't change the subject."

Kent tried his best to mimic the innocent look she always gave him. "Was there a subject?"

She knew what he was doing and she didn't appreciate it. "Yes, your ornery treatment of me."

Their eyes met and then he disarmed her completely by allowing a hint of a smile to twist his lips. "Ornery, huh? I don't seem to remember you complaining when we went off together last night."

Was he actually referring to it fondly? Maybe he was finally coming around. "Neither did you," Brianne pointed out.

"No, I didn't. Wasn't anything to complain about," he said matter-of-factly. He might have been talking about a successful roundup of the calves, until he added, "When you're not moving those lips too fast, they can be pretty sweet."

Lack of sleep made her take offense at the first part of his statement rather than comfort from the second half. "I need more coffee."

Kent raised his eyes from his plate. "What you need," he said firmly, "is sleep."

She couldn't really argue with that. "I'll turn in early tonight."

It became a contest of wills. "You'll turn in now."

Surprised, Brianne turned around. "I'm going with you."

Didn't this woman have a lick of sense in that head of hers? "No, you're not. If I thought you were a liability before, that goes double now."

One hand on her hip, Brianne narrowed her eyes. So much for thinking she'd made any headway at all with this Neanderthal in leather boots and worn jeans. "Since you were wrong before, does that go double now?"

He struggled not to raise his voice. "I'm not having you fall off your horse."

Was that his way of saying he was worried about her? "Don't worry, I won't sue you."

"No, but you'll slow me down."

She might have known. He wasn't worried about her, he was worried about his damn schedule. "Nice to know you're concerned."

Forgetting himself, Kent took hold of her shoulders. He was sorely tempted to give her a good shake. Something had to rattle that brain of hers into place. "Yeah, I'm concerned. Damn concerned."

Her chin shot up. "About the ranch."

Her chin made a hell of a good target. He restrained himself. "I already told you that." Kent paused, knowing he would regret this. But it came out just the same. "And about you." He loosened his hold and slid his hands down along her arms.

Brianne stared at him, afraid to allow herself to

believe he was saying what she thought he was saying. What she wanted him to say. "Me?"

Impatient with himself for not holding his ground, Kent gestured about the empty kitchen. "Do you see anyone else in this room I could be talking to?"

Slowly, she shook her head from side to side. The headache was still there, but Brianne hardly noticed. "No."

His face was completely devoid of expression. "Then it's you."

She needed this spelled out, not because she was trying to be difficult, but because she really wanted to be sure. "Let me get this straight. You're afraid I'll hurt myself?"

Kent had never liked having his back to the wall. Never liked being pinned down. "Woman, you're making a production out of this. Just stay out of my way and stay home. You can take all the pictures you want tomorrow when I don't have to keep looking over my shoulder to make sure the cattle haven't trampled you."

Miraculously, the fog was lifting from her brain. Holding up one hand, she ticked off reasons why she didn't have to remain behind, other than the fact that she refused to.

"A, you're not going on a cattle drive so we're not talking about a lot of cattle. B, I can stay up two, three days running if I have to. I've done it before. And C, this is a free country and I can do whatever I want to."

Kent was willing to bet that if Brianne had been

Daniel Webster, the devil wouldn't have lasted three acts before he was defeated. He would have run screaming from the courtroom once she wound herself up.

"The country may be free," he agreed tersely, "but the ranch is private. What I say here, goes. Check."

Oh, no, the game wasn't over that easily. "It's in your father's name. What *he* says, goes. Checkmate."

He fought hard to hold on to his temper. Unleashing it had never solved anything—even if it might make him feel good for the moment. "Damn it, you are the most stubborn woman God ever created."

"I have to be," she countered, though she was smiling when she said it, "to put up with you."

Put up with him? He was the one putting up with her, not the other way around. "Well, that won't be for much longer."

"No, it won't," she agreed, ignoring the sharp pinch of sadness she felt. "Now eat your damn breakfast so we can get on with it."

He eyed the plate. He'd only eaten half, even though it was good. Talking about her leaving had inexplicably taken away his appetite. "You don't have to keep sneaking in here and cooking breakfast for me, you know."

"I don't sneak." She rinsed off her own plate. "And what's the matter, afraid you'll get used to it?"

"Yeah."

His answer caught her off guard. She turned around to make sure she'd heard right. "What?"

Kent hadn't meant to say that. It had just slipped out. "I said I'm finished." He rose, abandoning his plate. He waited, knowing that she'd pick it up. "Let's go."

Quickly, she threw away the remains and rinsed off his dish. "Never give an inch, do you?" The plate clinked into place beside hers on the draining rack.

"Not unless it's cut out of me."

"Then you're safe." She fell into step beside him. "I don't cut."

"Yeah, you do." The mark she left on him threatened to go deeper than any knife wound. Their eyes met. "Get your hat. It's going to be a hot one today."

As if it'd been anything else these last few days. "Nice to know we're in for a change," she quipped.

He watched her walk ahead of him, his attention momentarily diverted by the rhythmic sway of her hips. "Not hardly," he murmured.

The morning seemed endless. The sun was high in the sky when Kent finally stepped back, and the last of the calves they'd rounded up today was led away. He was through branding for the day.

He caught a glimpse of Brianne's face. She looked pale. He knew he shouldn't have let her come along. "You all right?"

"I'm fine." She wiped her forehead with the back

of the glove she had on. Her expression softened slightly when she looked at him. "Thanks for asking."

He looked to see if any of the men had overheard, but they all seemed to be otherwise occupied. "Don't want you to spook the cattle when you fall off your horse."

She merely laughed. "You warm my heart, Kent."

He was already turning his hand to the next chore. "Wasn't my intention."

No, she thought, packing up her camera again, it probably wasn't.

But it'd happened just the same.

9

"Brianne, I want you to go back with John."

Brianne looked at Kent in surprise. They'd been out on the range all day and were just about to head back home. One of the men, Jack Russell, was about to take the plunge and get married this Sunday. That was just two days away and his friends were giving him one last taste of bachelorhood tonight at Serendipity's only saloon, appropriately named the Last Chance. Everyone was anxious to get back and put the dust of the day behind them.

Just before they mounted up, one of the men had taken Kent aside. The conversation was brief. She had no doubt that was Kent's doing. While the men all seemed inclined to drawl and lengthen any story they told, Kent's conversational style was spartan. It was as if each word he traded with someone came from his private stock and he didn't want to deplete it.

When the man had pointed off toward the horizon, Kent nodded. The next moment, he was returning for his horse. Curious, Brianne waited until he was within a few feet of her before she attempted to fire off any questions at him.

She didn't get the chance. He beat her at her own game and issued the thinly veiled order for her to leave with one of the older hands.

Brianne looked over her shoulder at John. The man looked uncomfortable about being caught in the middle. "Aren't you coming?" she asked Kent.

Kent checked the condition of his saddlebags. He'd packed nonperishables earlier in the week, just in case. He'd learned a long time ago that you had to be prepared for anything out here. He scarcely spared her a look.

"No."

The man was a font of information. Brianne tried to pin him down. "Where are you going?"

Kent still didn't care to be questioned, but he supposed it did no harm to tell her. He tightened the ties holding his bedroll in place.

"Some of the calves have strayed off from the main herd." He nodded toward one of the cowboys he'd been talking to. "Simms just did a count. I'm going to go look for them."

It sounded reasonable enough to her. Brianne picked up her reins. "All right, let's get started."

Where had she gotten the idea that she was coming along? He'd just told her to go home. Kent caught Brianne's hand before she could mount her horse. "I'm not going on a picnic, woman."

Were they going to have this fight again? Brianne

had thought by now they'd reached an understanding about the nature of her involvement. Apparently not.

"That's good," she replied, just as sarcastically, "because I didn't pack a picnic lunch."

"You're not going," he insisted with a note of finality that would have made any of his men back away. All it seemed to do was spur Brianne on. "I might be out the better part of the night."

Why would he think that would put her off? Brianne wondered. "I'm not afraid of the dark."

He bit back a curse. "You don't have enough sense to be afraid of anything."

She looked Kent square in the eye, knowing it irritated him. The fact that some of the hands were looking on didn't make her back off. She'd gotten to know most of them and felt as if she'd even struck up a few friendships.

"Oh, I'm afraid of things, Kent. Just not the dark." Her eyes met his. "Or you. Now, do I come with you, or do I trail behind? Because one way or another, I am going."

He'd let her come to the brandings, let her follow him around like a damn shadow when they mended fences and herded the cattle. What more did she want from him? When was she going to be satisfied?

"Why the hell would you want to go?" he demanded.

He still didn't get it, did he? Brianne thought. "Because I'm recording everything that has to do with ranching and looking for strays is part of it."

Kent was going alone and he didn't want her tagging along after him. Not because it was particularly dangerous or even because it was boring, but because he didn't want to spend that much time alone with her. It was hard enough just having her near him day after day with the men around.

Exasperated, he checked his rifle. He'd heard there'd been mountain lion sightings and he wasn't going to take any chances. "Didn't any of those other guys you haunted go looking for strays?"

Brianne looked up at him serenely. "They never lost any."

He made a comment that she knew she could never quote in her article. John, still standing beside her like an awkward appendage, cleared his throat and slanted a glance in her direction to see her reaction. Brianne merely laughed at the expletive. "Do you kiss your mother with that mouth?"

Strangling her in front of so many witnesses was a bad idea, even if they were his own men. Disgusted, Kent turned away and put his foot in the stirrup. "John, take her to my parents' house, even if you have to tie her up and sling her over the saddle to do it."

John exchanged glances with some of the men close enough to hear, then looked uncertainly at Brianne. She was smiling at him, but any fool could see that there was an edge to the smile.

"Touch me, John," she warned, still smiling, "and you'll live to regret it."

That was enough for him. John raised his hands in complete surrender, not doubting her threat for a moment. Backing away, he looked at Kent. "Not me, boss. Uh-uh. I'd rather ride bareback on Ol' Blue," he swore, referring to the prize Black Angus bull they'd recently purchased for breeding.

Brianne grinned. "Sounds interesting. Which of you would be bareback?" To her delight, she actually saw John's face turn as red as the bandanna that was hanging out of his back pocket.

Several of the men laughed at the thought of John, whose physique resembled a tall telephone pole, buck naked. Some things, Kent thought, were best left unexplored.

Meanwhile, they were losing daylight.

"Never mind," Kent told her, giving up. "If you're coming, come on. Otherwise, head back with John."

"I'm coming." As far as she was concerned, there'd never been any doubt.

Brianne swung into her saddle with a grace Kent had to grudgingly admire. She got under his skin almost constantly, for more reasons than he cared to consider, but there was no denying that the lady sat a horse as pretty as poetry.

Without saying a word to her, he pressed his heels against Whiskey and turned the horse toward the north. Brianne turned her horse to follow, urging the animal on quickly in order to catch up. She knew Kent would make no allowances for her. No doubt, if she fell into a snake pit, he'd just keep right on going without breaking stride.

By the time she drew up alongside him, she realized that there were just the two of them going after the strays. "Why aren't you taking anyone else with you?"

Why did she have to question everything? He was tired of explaining his every movement to her. "Because they're all heading into town. Russell's getting married come Sunday and they're throwing him a bachelor party."

She already knew that. Jack Russell and Kent were as close as Kent allowed himself to be with anyone. Why wasn't he going? "Aren't you invited to the party?"

Kent squinted, trying to make out something in the distance. He muttered under his breath when he realized it was just a rock formation. He might have known it wasn't going to be that easy.

"Yeah, I was invited to the party."

Brianne heard annoyance framing each word. "But you're not going." It wasn't a question.

Turning Whiskey in a more northwesterly direction, he didn't bother looking in her direction. "I told you before, I don't like crowds."

His feelings about crowds had nothing to do with it. Crowds were people you didn't know. "But these are your hands." She studied his stony profile when he made no comment. "You'd go to that party if it weren't for the missing calves, wouldn't you?"

"Don't you ever run out of questions?"

She pretended to think that over, then said brightly, "No."

"Well, I'm out of answers."

She shrugged. "You don't have to answer, I know the answer already."

Kent didn't like the smug way she thought she had his number. If he chose to go after the calves alone, or almost alone, that was his business, not hers. "Oh, you do, do you?"

"Yes." She urged her horse on a little faster so she could get a better look at Kent's face. "I'm on to you, Kent Cutler. You're not as tough as you'd like me to believe."

He purposely moved ahead to put an end to her scrutiny. "What you believe or don't believe really doesn't interest me."

"I don't believe that, either."

Her laughter enveloped him. How could one sound be sexy and irritating as hell at the same time? "Why?"

"Because your brother told me that you're an all-or-nothing kind of man. Men like that don't just kiss and walk away." She raised her voice as he moved further ahead of her. "That means if they kiss a woman, they invest a little of themselves."

What was that supposed to mean? And where did she get off discussing him with anyone? He slowed his horse, waiting for her to catch up. When she did, he demanded, "Which brother?"

From this vantage point, colored by the haze of a punch that lived up to its name, Sunday night had begun to run together. She wasn't sure if it was Hank or Will who had told her. "Does it matter?"

"It will to them, if I have to beat the living daylights out of all of them to get at the right guy," he answered matter-of-factly.

She couldn't visualize the Cutler brothers going at it like some homeless street fighters, battling it out for a place to rest out of the rain.

"For telling the truth?" she challenged.

He wasn't about to debate with her whether or not it was the truth. She wouldn't be satisfied until she drew blood and obviously would rather die than surrender. Since Quint was the sheriff in Serendipity, a homicide in the family might prove to be embarrassing.

So he growled, "Woman, would it be too much to ask for you to stop exercising that mouth of yours for a while so I could get my mind back on finding those calves before nightfall?"

As if anything could deter him from his goal, Brianne thought. He was the most single-minded person she'd ever met. "Oh, that's right, I interfere with your thinking."

He shot her an accusing look. "You're smirking again."

"Smiling, Kent, smiling," she corrected for the umpteenth time. "Someday, maybe you'll learn the difference."

He banked down the emotions the comment raised. There wasn't going to be a someday. "You won't be around for 'someday,' remember?"

"Right." The lack of emotion in his voice stung, Brianne realized. It meant nothing to him that she was leaving. He didn't care if they never saw one another again. She was accustomed to harmless flirtations, truly enjoyed flirting with men and being flirted with. But what might have started out that way had somehow gotten completely misdirected and sidetracked.

She wanted him to feel something for her, the way she felt for him. That he didn't seem to bothered her more than she could possibly put into words.

Better to get her mind back on the reason they were out here. Sparring with Kent had lost its appeal.

Brianne looked around slowly. Scores of men could get lost here, never mind a handful of calves. It was like looking for a needle in the proverbial haystack. The countryside stretched out endlessly before her, lush and beautiful. And lonely.

She looked at Kent. "Got any ideas where they might be?"

"Wouldn't be out here if I didn't."

"Yeah, you would." He shot her a look, not knowing if she was going to follow her words with another sarcastic gibe or not. "Like the stubborn man you are, you'd look everywhere just to bring those calves back."

Well, at least she had that right, Kent thought. "Because they belong to the Shady Lady."

Brianne was beginning to believe that there was more to it than that. It wasn't just about property. He cared. At least about lost cattle. "Because they're lost."

She couldn't put a label on the look he gave her. The best way to describe it was to say that there was surprise in it, as if she'd managed to unlock a door he didn't want tampered with.

Kent attempted to shrug off the meaning behind her comment. He didn't want her making a big deal out of this. Or out of anything he was doing. He was just doing his job.

"Cattle are precious. You don't want any dying if you can help it."

It wasn't as simple as that, Brianne thought. He had that extra something when it came to running the ranch that put him above the others. "You're a good man, Kent, even if you don't want anyone knowing it."

There she went again, acting as if she knew him inside and out. She had no business trying to fit him in a niche. He was just Kent Cutler, nothing more, nothing less.

"Are you going to stop waving those lips of yours anytime soon?"

"No, not anytime soon," she repeated. Brianne caught her tongue between her teeth, grinned, then added, "I know all the words to maybe some two hundred songs and some of the words to several hundred more. When I run out of things to talk about, I sing."

The groan was heartfelt. "I should have hog-tied you to that saddle myself."

She laughed at the threat. "You and what army?"

The woman was not to be believed. He stared at her. "Now you're telling me that you think you're stronger than I am?"

She wasn't being stupid, or irrational. "Not stronger, just more agile. You don't have to be strong to beat someone at their own game, you just have to be alert and watch for an opening."

Kent hadn't a clue how to respond to that, so he said nothing. A man knew his limitations, and though it rankled him, he knew that he absolutely was no match for that mouth of hers.

No, no match at all, he thought looking at it, no matter how she used it.

"Shouldn't we be getting back?" They'd been at this for over two hours and it was getting dark. There was still no trace of the missing calves.

He hated to admit it, but maybe she was right. Grudgingly, Kent turned his horse around when something caught his attention. He remained ramrod still, listening intently.

Brianne had seen the same look on her father's dog when the animal detected a sound far away that the rest of them couldn't begin to hear. She strained her ears but couldn't pick up a thing.

"What is it?"

He didn't answer. Instead, Kent kicked his heels into Whiskey's flanks and urged the quarter horse on at a fast clip.

"All right, don't tell me," she muttered gamely.

Turning, Brianne followed Kent and caught up within a few lengths. It didn't take long before she heard it too. The plaintive lowing of cattle. It was a mournful, pathetic sound.

"You found them."

The look he spared her indicated that he'd never doubted he would. Had he been alone, the idea of going back without them wouldn't have entered his mind. It was only her presence that had made him waver.

"It's what I set out to do."

The man had been raised on too many Gary Cooper movies, she thought. "Is it normal for cattle to stray this far from the herd?"

Kent didn't allow Whiskey to break stride until they'd reached the prodigal calves. The animals, five in number, had come perilously close to drifting over a ravine. He'd found them just in time.

"The wind shifts, they can't smell the herd, so they just keep wandering and looking." Getting Whiskey in front of the animals, he turned the calves in a southeasterly direction. Toward home. From what he could see, they were none the worse for their adventure.

The pace slackened. Kent obviously didn't want to take a chance on the calves spooking and running off. Brianne smiled. No people skills to speak of, but the man was kind to animals. It was something.

So was accomplishing what he'd set out to do. He'd found his five needles in the haystack. "Well, I have to say that I'm impressed."

The compliment nudged at something warm within him. He tried vainly to ignore it. He didn't need her stamp of approval to know he'd accomplished something. "Didn't do it to impress you."

"Nothing is clearer to me than that, believe me. But I can still be impressed."

Brianne looked up. There was a silvery cloud stretched across the bottom half of the moon like a worn feathered boa. Darkness was quickly enshrouding them. She didn't doubt that Kent had eyes like a cat, but traveling at night still made her a little uneasy.

There were coyotes and mountain lions in these parts, not to mention rattlers. The darkness made them more formidable.

"Are we going to herd them back in the dark?"

Was it his imagination, or did she sound nervous? "Don't you think I can?"

He'd said "I," not "we," Brianne realized. As far as he was concerned, she hadn't proven herself at all. He saw her strictly as an observer, not an asset. It was more than just her competitive nature that was bothered by that.

"I think you could probably shoe horses with your bare hands if you put your mind to it, but under normal circumstances, wouldn't you bed the herdlet down for the night?"

"Herdlet?" he echoed incredulously. "What the hell kind of word is that?"

She grinned, knowing it was useless to tell him that she liked coining words to fit the occasion. "Five calves don't make a herd."

He was glad to prove her wrong. "They did for my great-great-grandfather. That's how the Shady

Lady Ranch got started. With five calves, a scrap of land and a dream.''

Color, legend, all coming out of Kent. She could hardly believe it. ''Tell me about it.''

Even in the faded moonlight, she could see that Kent was looking at her as if she were simpleminded. ''I just did.''

''The long version,'' she insisted.

He sighed. Why was she always trying to drag things out of him that weren't there? Like feelings, feelings that he didn't have anymore. Feelings that he refused to have anymore.

''My father's better at it than I am.''

She wasn't going to let him evade her. They were out here together and all they had was time. ''I'm not asking your father, I'm asking you.''

''Well, you should be asking my father. I'm no good at embellishing stories, or saying things women want to hear.'' He looked at her to make sure she understood his meaning. He couldn't tell her what she needed to hear. What she deserved to hear. It wasn't in him. ''I do what I do well and I know my limits. You want stories, you talk to someone else.''

''I don't want to talk to someone else.'' She looked at him significantly. ''I want to talk to you.''

He looked away, weighing his options. They could be back at the main house in a couple of hours, provided they didn't run into any coyotes or unaccommodating mountain lions. It was the thought of the latter that made up his mind for him. He didn't want to take a chance on losing the calves after finding them. Or her.

"We'll stay here until morning." He reined in, then looked at her. "Any objections?"

He was actually asking her? Brianne wondered if she'd fallen asleep in the saddle and was dreaming. "I don't mind sleeping out beneath the stars." She was no stranger to camping out. "It's my last night here, it'd be nice to do something a little different."

"Your last night?" A distant emptiness nudged him. Ignoring it wasn't as easy as he would have liked. Dismounting, he looked at her incredulously. "I thought you weren't leaving until sometime Saturday."

Brianne began to loosen the cinch to her saddle. Was that surprise or happiness she heard in his voice? "I'm not. But I'm spending the last twenty-four hours in Serendipity to get some background information and photographs for the article." Quint had offered to put her up for the night and she had accepted. She dragged the saddle off and placed it on the ground. "See, I'm going to be out of your hair sooner than you thought." She glanced toward him. "That should make you very happy."

Funny, Kent didn't exactly feel happy. He wasn't sure what he was feeling, other than being taken by surprise. "It'll make things easier."

Brianne should have known better. She'd given him so many openings, so many opportunities to say something, anything, that would give her the slightest indication he wanted her to return when she was finished putting her article to bed. There was even a reason to return—Hank and Fiona's wedding. But Kent hadn't taken a single hint.

No man was that obtuse. The plain and simple fact was that he didn't want her to come back. There was no use beating her head against a stone wall.

Kent collected enough rocks to encircle a small fire. Just enough to keep any nocturnal creatures in the vicinity at bay. Striking a match, he squatted down and carefully coaxed the flame until it nestled within the kindling. "Are you hungry?"

Feeling oddly hollow, Brianne ran her hands along her arms. The temperature was dropping now that the sun had set. "What?"

"Food." He dusted his hands off on his jeans. "Do you want any?"

She stared at him uncomprehendingly. "You brought food with you?"

What did she expect? "This isn't New York, with a deli on every other corner. Out here, you have to be prepared for anything." He nodded toward his saddlebags. "I've got some beef jerky and a can of beans."

The selection didn't surprise her. "A meal fit for a king."

Was she looking down her nose at him? "Hey, when you're hungry—"

God, he was so quick to take offense. "It'll do fine." Brianne eyed the saddlebag as he took the provisions out. "I don't suppose you have something in there that passes for a mattress."

He untied his bedroll. "I've got a blanket."

"Just the one?" It was a rhetorical question.

He tossed it on the ground beside her saddle. The saddle could serve as a pillow. "That's all it takes. I wasn't expecting you to come along," he reminded her. "You can have it."

Just when she'd stuck an unflattering label on him, he turned noble on her. "But it's yours."

Why was everything an argument with this woman? "And I can give it away if I want to." He pulled out the small pan from the saddlebag. He'd warm the beans in that. It wouldn't be much of a dinner, but it would have to do.

She wasn't about to have him remember that he'd gotten sick because of her.

"We can share it." She saw the wary look that came into his eyes. "Don't worry, I can be respectable when I have to be." Turning from him, she began to spread out the bedroll.

Damn it, didn't she understand yet that she was a weakness he was trying to conquer? "Wasn't you I was worrying about."

Brianne raised her eyes from the blanket. "Oh?"

"Wipe that grin off your face, Gainsborough. After all, I'm only made out of flesh and blood."

She rose to stand before him. "Since this is the last night you'll have to put up with me, do you think you could find it in your heart to call me by my first name?"

All things considered, he'd rather not bring his heart into this. "Why?"

"Because I'd like to hear you say it, just once."

Feeling like a trick pony at the fair, he sighed, then mumbled, "Brianne."

He would have said the name of bathroom cleanser with more affection. "Again."

It came out softer this time. "Brianne."

She let it waft along her consciousness. "Now I know why you never said it before."

Maybe he wasn't thinking quite clearly, but he couldn't quite bring himself to step away. "Why?"

"Because it makes you smile when you do." She laced her arms around his neck. "You have a very nice smile, you know."

He didn't know anything of the kind. And he certainly didn't know what he was doing here, like this with her. All he knew was that given a choice, there was no other place he would want to be but here, with her.

Kent glanced over her shoulder at the provisions he'd unpacked. "Are you very hungry?"

She was, but not for food. "No."

This time, there was no one to come up behind them and interrupt. This time, they were all alone.

The food could wait, Kent thought. "Neither am I."

Everything within her body became alert. And melted the next moment when he took her into his arms. She watched his eyes for as long as she could, until her own eyes closed. But Brianne didn't believe in kissing with her eyes open. It took some of the magic away.

And she didn't want to take a chance on losing even a single ray.

10

➤ ◆ ◄

All the doubts she'd had about his feelings vanished into the darkness of the night. A man without feelings couldn't make love like this. Couldn't bring her so swiftly, so skillfully to the center of a tempest of emotions.

As his mouth moved over her body, as she arched and ached for more, Brianne felt as if she'd never made love before. In her heart, she knew that nothing she'd ever experienced had ever come close and nothing would ever be as wondrous as this again.

Unless it was with him.

Though he would never have said it out loud, and certainly not to her, Kent felt as if he'd been touched by magic. Magic that unlocked something within him he had no power of unlocking himself. He'd felt dead all this time, dead and barren of feelings, and certain that there was nothing left within him that was capable of responding to a woman to this degree.

He'd been wrong.

The moment he touched his mouth to hers, the moment they came together on that sorry, threadbare blanket of his, feelings rushed out, bathing him in their intensity. Drenching him as wave after wave overcame any remnant of resistance he might have had to offer.

Making love with Brianne had turned out to be even more of a volatile, explosive experience than he had thought it would be.

For the span of one endless night, he shed the shackles that had been holding him prisoner and lost himself in freedom. Freedom to feel without the threat of pain finding him.

And when it was over, when he'd spent every molecule of energy that his body had to give, Kent rolled off her slick, near liquid form and gathered Brianne to him, content to feel just the heat of her body against his.

And to pretend that morning wouldn't come looking for them.

He inhaled deeply, trying to catch his breath, to make it steady again. The scent in her hair filled his head. Stirred his body. Damn, but the lady was lethal.

"You made enough noise to spook the cattle," he murmured, his lips brushing against her temple.

She'd never felt so alive, so content and so exhausted all at the same time. For a while, she had even forgotten where she was, other than some place very special. Now, slowly, it was all coming back into focus.

She had been pretty noisy, she realized with a grin. Pleasure had exacted sounds of enjoyment from her. The happiness she felt just couldn't be contained within the boundaries of her body. She'd always been vocal about joy. And never more than tonight.

"Are they still here?" She couldn't even find the strength to turn and look.

He raised his head just enough to see the makeshift corral he'd strung around the five calves. "Yup." He grinned at her as he lay down again. "I think they're taking notes."

Brianne laughed. A sense of humor. There was hope for him yet. All this and heaven, too. With her last ounce of energy, she pressed a kiss to his shoulder. "Beats eating grass seven ways from sundown."

"Mmm?"

She felt his breath, warm and steady, against her throat, lingering along her breast. Maybe a tad too steady.

"Are you falling asleep on me?" The rhythmic sound of his breathing answered the question for her. Brianne laughed softly to herself. "No pun intended," she added. Taking care not to wake him, she shifted slightly so that his body could warm her during the night. "You make one hell of a throw rug, Cutler." She snuggled into place. "A girl couldn't ask for much more."

But in the morning, Brianne learned that she could. She could ask for a great deal more.

Like a man who acted as if they'd crossed a new threshold, rather than someone who pretended that everything was the same as it had been the day before. Someone who apparently preferred to think that what had happened in the night fell under the heading of a dream.

Her eyes still closed, Brianne had reached for him, wanting to snatch just a little more of the euphoria that had been so much a part of last night and hug it to her. But her hand had come in contact with only the empty blanket.

Sitting up, she looked around as she dragged the blanket around her. Kent was squatting down beside the dormant campfire, his back to her.

There was something in the rigid set of his shoulders that warned Brianne the man she'd made love with last night had retreated.

Still, maybe it was her imagination. "You're up and dressed," she commented, disappointed. A part of her had hoped to greet the morning the way she had ushered in the night.

He didn't turn around all the way. Still squatting, he aimed his words in her general direction. "Looks like I finally beat you to it."

The distance in his voice made her feel cold. The blanket was no defense against it. "I didn't realize it meant so much to you."

It didn't, he thought, but she did. And that was wrong. Wrong because it had nowhere to go.

He rose, sticking his hands into his back pockets. He kicked more dirt into the campfire, even though the flame had long since gone out. "I don't have any coffee."

"I can get started without it. I think," she added uncertainly. What she couldn't get past was the cool-

ness that was facing her. Why was he acting as if
they were barely acquainted strangers, instead of two
people who had discovered something rare and precious last night?

Why didn't he come over here and take her in his
arms, the way she ached for him to do?

His choice, she thought, galvanizing her resolve.
And, his loss. If the thought carried any further—to
her own loss—Brianne refused to go there.

She looked around, not really seeing anything, just
feeling the bitter sting of her own disappointment,
her own stupidity for thinking that one night could
change him.

Her clothes were in a heap beside the blanket; she
reached for them. "Guess I'd better get ready."

Kent glanced at her then, and had trouble looking
away. She was leaving today and he'd probably
never see her again. It made no sense to dwell on
what had happened last night. To think about it
would only make him feel empty now, empty at the
prospect of never feeling that alive again.

Kent nodded in response. "Unless you want to
ride back like that."

She thought she detected a hint of a smile, but
dismissed it. He wasn't human, he was a stone statue,
incapable of feelings. "I might get saddle sore."

Brianne rose to her feet, the blanket slipping from
her body as she reached for her clothes.

Kent's mouth fell open. He felt the muscles of his
body tightening, felt desire send a fresh salvo

through his veins. Was she trying to drive him crazy? Or just taunting him?

He turned away, his hands fisted so tightly he dug his nails into his palms. "What the hell are you doing?" he demanded angrily.

If she could have gotten her hands on a good-size rock, she would have thrown it him. "I'm getting dressed," she bit off.

He could see that, but why did she have to do it in front of him? Just how much self-control did she think he had?

"Don't you want to go behind a tree and do it?"

When she laughed, the sound low and sinfully lusty in its amusement, he almost turned around then. At that moment, he could have gotten down on his knees and begged her to stay, but he knew it would be no good. She belonged elsewhere far more than Rosemary ever had. Brianne had a home and a career waiting for her on the East Coast. He had nothing to offer that could compete with it and he wouldn't sacrifice his pride by asking her to stay with him. Not when he knew she'd say no.

He didn't deal with rejection very well.

"Wouldn't that be a little like fitting the barn door for a lock after the stallion had run off with the mare?" She smiled to herself at her own choice of words. "You've already seen me naked. I don't look any different in the daylight than I do in the dark."

Yes, she did, Kent thought. She looked better. His eyes trained in front of him, he put one foot in front of the other, not altogether sure how he managed. "I'll saddle the horses."

Stuffing her bra into her back pocket, she punched her arms through her shirt, buttoned enough buttons to be decent and tucked the tails into her jeans. "You do what you're good at," she replied flatly.

The words stopped him dead in his tracks. His own survival notwithstanding, his conscience chafed him for ending it this way. "Meaning?"

Brianne pulled on her boots. "Whatever you want it to mean." If he wanted to run, that was his problem, not hers. On her feet again, she strode up to him. "I'm dressed, you can stop being gallant. I'll saddle my own horse, thanks."

Maybe it was his imagination, but he thought he saw hurt in her eyes. "Brianne, I told you once nothing was going to come of this."

She wasn't going to be lectured on top of everything else. Being unceremoniously dumped was quite enough for one day.

And to think that she had actually thought he was sensitive.

Brianne raised her chin, her defenses braced. "Yes, you did, didn't you? And you're a man of your word, I'm sure."

Damn it, he didn't want to argue, he wanted to kiss her and hold her until the earth was just a faded memory in the sky.

His hands remained at his sides. "What are you so sore about?"

"I'm not sore," she snapped, afraid that tension

would loosen her tears and ruin everything. She wasn't going to let him think she was crying over him. "I'm tired. I need coffee."

And he needed her, but all that was moot. "So let's get these calves back in a hurry."

"Not fast enough for me," she muttered, throwing her saddle on the horse's back.

But too fast for him, he thought.

It was hard saying goodbye. Hard because she'd truly come to like Jake and Zoe Cutler, liked being around them. They were her own fairy-tale parents come to life. If her mother had lived, Brianne knew that her parents would have behaved just the way Kent's did, with a comfortable, knowing affection underlining everything they did.

And it was equally hard leaving because she truly felt that she'd fit in on the ranch. She'd enjoyed all of it, the challenge of every day, the work, the land, the camaraderie of the men. Always outgoing and gregarious, Brianne had made more friends here in the short time she'd been at the Shady Lady than she usually did. She'd certainly gotten along marvelously with the Cutler men.

Save for one.

Kent was conspicuously absent from the ring of people as Brianne said her goodbyes. He'd dropped off the calves, and mumbled something about checking a length of fencing. Then he rode off before she could say a word.

She might not have been able to say anything, but

no such problem plagued Jake. He had several things to say about his son's abrupt behavior, none of it flattering. For once, Zoe didn't come to Kent's defense.

Brianne pretended it didn't matter, though she caught herself more than once looking in the direction he'd ridden off. Hoping.

She shrugged in response to Jake's last criticism as she watched him load her equipment into the rented vehicle. "Maybe he's busy celebrating the fact that I won't be following him around anymore."

Jake snorted. "If he is, then he's no son of mine." He looked at Brianne. Part of him had hoped that, perhaps, she would become part of the family in name as well as in spirit. "If I were his age, I wouldn't be celebrating a beautiful girl leaving. I'd be doing my damnedest to make her stay."

The heated declaration did wonders for her bruised ego. Brianne leaned over and kissed Jake's cheek.

"Knew I liked you the first minute I met you." She looked at Zoe and saw an understanding in the woman's eyes that almost undid her. She knew, Brianne thought. Knew how she felt. "Say goodbye for me, will you? And tell him…tell him that I appreciate everything he did because I know how hard it was for him to let me into his world."

But not so hard to slam the door again, she thought bitterly. She rallied, then smiled broadly. "I'll send you all copies of the magazine once it's out."

Zoe slipped an arm around Brianne's shoulders

and gave her a light squeeze. "Sure you don't want one of us coming into town with you?"

Brianne shook her head. "You've both put yourselves out for me more than enough." She struggled to keep her voice level. Goodbyes were something she'd always hated. "Thank you for making me feel like one of the family."

Zoe smiled sadly. Kent had some tall accounting to do when she got her hands on him. "It wasn't hard at all," she assured Brianne.

After saying a final goodbye to the wranglers, who had gathered around the main house, Brianne got into the car and drove off toward Serendipity.

She had no way of knowing that as she passed a large ridge on her way to town, a lone rider watched her progress and silently said his own goodbyes.

"You keep grooming him like that, you're going to have the only skinless horse around."

Kent never broke rhythm as he continued brushing Whiskey in his stall. He didn't bother turning around. He didn't have to. He knew it was Quint from the first word his brother uttered.

He should have known better than to hang around here. The range was the only place to be when a man wanted to be alone. "What are you doing here?"

Quint walked into the stall. "A simple hello would be nice."

"Hello."

The greeting was more of a growl than a word. Quint stroked Whiskey's muzzle. So, it was as bad as people said, he thought, glancing at his brother. Kent's profile was wooden as he continued brushing.

Quint leaned back against the stall and studied his younger brother. "Ma called and asked me to stop by and talk to you."

Talk. Talking wouldn't accomplish anything. That was something *she* would have suggested. Always moving her mouth, Kent thought angrily, taking another long, sweeping pass over Whiskey's rear flanks with his brush.

"Why?"

Quint laughed shortly. The question was rhetorical for everyone but Kent. "I think you know why. You've never had the most easygoing temperament." He shrugged, looking around. Kent had fixed up the stable some. The last time he remembered being in here, it had been in disrepair. Kent was too good a man to waste his life married to a ranch. "The rest of us figured it was something that just developed because you'd had to fight so hard to hang on as a little guy." Quint moved forward to face him. Kent kept his eyes on the horse. "But you've hung on quite a few years, and you're not a little guy any longer. Ma says you've been a mean, ugly son of a bitch these last two weeks."

Kent looked up in surprise.

"Oh, those weren't her exact words, but that was what she meant." Kent gave him a disgusted look and said nothing, as he went back to brushing his horse. Quint tried again. "Will said he stopped by the other day and you almost took his head clean off when he asked you if you'd heard from Brianne.''

Kent's jaw hardened. He wished everyone would just butt out and leave him alone. "Well, I hadn't. And there's no reason why I should have."

This time, the laugh had no feeling behind it, save for pity. "You believe that, you're dumber than a post. And you're not a post."

Kent's thin hold on his temper all but gave out. "Look, she's gone back to New York. I'm here, she's there. End of story."

His brother had the tenacity of a pit bull when he set his mind to something. They'd all seen proof of that here at the Shady Lady. "Only if you want it to be."

Disgust turned the corners of his mouth down. "I don't have anything to say about it."

"That'd be a first." Kent always made his opinion known, in one way or another. Sympathy softened his voice as Quint laid a hand on his shoulder. "Why don't you pick up a phone and call her?"

Mechanically, Kent shrugged his brother off and went on working. "Don't have the number."

That was a cop-out and they both knew it. "There's always directory assistance. Oh, I forgot, you don't take assistance, do you?"

Kent struggled not to rail at the sarcasm. He didn't like feeling as if he wasn't in control, and that included losing his temper. Although in his book Quint was asking for it.

"I don't like talking on the phone."

"You don't like very much of anything lately, do you?" Quint observed. What did it take to get Kent to admit he'd made a mistake in letting her go?

Kent moved to the other side of the horse and started the process over again. "I especially don't like older brothers thinking that they have a right to interfere in my life."

"What life?" Quint very rarely lost his temper, but now he felt it beginning to fray. "Cattle aren't a life, kid. A wife, kids, that's a life."

"Don't call me kid." Kent's eyes darkened as he glared at Quint over Whiskey's shoulder. "And you should talk."

"Yeah, I should." He wouldn't mind settling down. Quint was at an age where the idea had a great deal of appeal. But wanting and doing were two very different things. Doing had certain requirements. "I just haven't found the right one."

For a second, Kent stopped grooming Whiskey, but then he resumed brushing again. "And what makes you think I have?"

A simpleton would have noticed. "The look in your eyes when you looked at her. The glare in them when you saw me talking to her and thought I was moving in on your territory."

Kent was getting damn tired of people acting as if they knew what was best for him. What was best was just to be left alone so he could come to terms with his life. To get it back to where it had been before *she* came and turned it all on its ear.

"I don't know what you're talking about." He

threw down the brush and turned to face Quint. "I don't have any territory."

"No, and you won't," Quint agreed evenly, "if you don't file your claim to it. There're a lot of claim-jumpers out there. One of them's bound to stake a claim if you don't. She's prime stuff—"

Quint's irreverent observation struck the wrong chord. Frustrated, angry and pushed past his limit, Kent took a swing at his brother, connecting with Quint's chin. Quint, more surprised than injured, staggered back several feet before he caught himself. His hands immediately fisted, but common sense prevailed, holding him back.

"Because you're my brother and obviously not yourself, I'll let that one go. But only this once," he warned. Quint rubbed his chin. "Now instead of taking your frustrations out on me, I suggest you do something smart for a change, ask Dad for her old man's number and go look the lady up. Otherwise, I just might have to put you in jail for your own good, before you hurt somebody else."

Kent knew Quint wasn't referring to himself. "Who've I hurt?"

Quint shook his head. "If you don't know the answer to that, then you're a lot slower than I thought you were."

As he turned to pick up the brush Kent had thrown, Quint heard the stable door close. He smiled as he slowly began brushing Whiskey's coat, then winced as a pain shot from his jaw straight up to his eyes. The kid had a harder punch than he did.

"Took him long enough, didn't it, Whiskey?"

The horse nudged his hand, the one with the brush in it. With a satisfied laugh, Quint resumed brushing.

Brianne stared at the computer screen on her desk. It was blank.

Just like her mind.

The photographs she'd taken this last month and a half had all been developed, tagged and pored over. With some outside input, she'd made her choices. All that remained was to write the piece.

All. The word mocked her.

The first two-thirds had gone well enough, but she'd come to a grinding halt at the last section.

Kent's section.

Stymied, she'd abandoned trying to work at home. The quiet was driving her crazy. But coming to the office hadn't helped, either. The noise of a magazine actively being put together surrounded her, but all it did was make it harder for her to concentrate.

Who was she kidding? She couldn't concentrate no matter where she went.

That damn cowboy had destroyed her power of concentration, of creativity. Something else to blame him for, in addition to her sleepless nights and her loss of appetite.

Brianne closed her eyes. She needed a vacation, a long one. From everything. Including her own thoughts.

Her phone buzzed and she jumped. She stared at it.

Oh, please, don't let it be Simon.

The editor had been calling her periodically, asking if she was finished yet. Hers was the last outstanding article before the magazine was put to bed.

She'd never been late before. It just wasn't like her.

Nothing was like her since she'd returned.

Damn Kent Cutler anyway.

She jerked up the telephone receiver. "Gainsborough."

"Ms. Gainsborough?" The halting voice of the receptionist was hardly audible. "There's a man out here asking to see you. No, wait, please," she suddenly cried. "You're not supposed to go in there—"

"Linda? Linda, who is it?" But instead of an answer, Brianne thought she heard someone calling her name. Yelling it, actually. Startled, her heart quickening in her chest, Brianne rose and looked over the top of her cubicle wall.

"I don't know," Linda's voice blurted from the receiver. "Some—"

"—Cowboy," Brianne concluded for her.

She didn't believe it. Kent was striding through the maze of cubicles, looking over the top of each one. The same expression on his face as when he'd gone after the calves.

"Should I call security?" the receptionist asked uncertainly.

"No, don't do that," Brianne ordered, then lowered her voice a decibel. "I won't be needing them." She let the receiver fall back into the cradle. He looked like a bull ready to charge. Anticipation went from a whisper to a roar as she signaled to him. "Over here."

Her mouth felt dry as she watched him approach. Kent was scowling, just the way he'd been the first time she saw him.

What was he doing here? She was afraid to even form a guess.

He seemed to take up all the room within her cubicle when he entered. "A little far from the ranch, aren't you?"

Kent didn't bother answering that. It took everything he had not to throw his arms around her and pull her to him. Damn, but he had no idea he could miss someone so much. "You forgot something."

She watched his eyes, searching. He gave nothing away. "What?"

"This." He took a photograph out of his pocket and tossed it on her desk. It was slightly bent, as if it had traveled in his pocket a while.

Brianne looked down at the photograph. It was of the two of them, dancing at Hank and Fiona's party. A slightly out-of-focus shot Will had taken. She'd treasured it the moment he'd handed it to her. She wasn't accustomed to people taking pictures of her, only the other way around.

Gently, as if it would disappear if she mishandled it, Brianne picked it up. "Thanks. I looked all over for that."

"It was under your bed. Ma found it." He didn't add that it had been placed on his coffee table where he was sure to see it. Didn't tell her that looking at it had been what had sent him so far over the edge that he'd booked a flight for New York.

Brianne nodded, still holding the photograph. "Thank her for me."

"You can do that yourself," he informed her.

Seeing him like this had thrown her brain into slow motion. "Right. Of course. I'll call her."

But Kent shook his head. "Over dinner."

Brianne interpreted that the only way she could. "She's here?"

"No."

Confused, she stared at him. If Zoe hadn't flown in with him, how could she possibly thank the woman over dinner? "Then how—?"

What little space there was in the cubicle disappeared as he took a step toward her. "You can be at the Shady Lady in five hours. In time for dinner. She's saving a place for you."

Brianne felt her knees suddenly turn rubbery. She pressed her hip against the side of the desk. "Why would she be doing that?"

He couldn't help himself any longer. Maybe it made him less of a man in her eyes, but it didn't matter. He had to hold her. Now. "Because I told her I was bringing you back."

A small circle of warmth began growing within her chest. "Oh, you did, did you?"

"Yeah." He snapped the word out, but there was a tenderness in his eyes she'd only seen that last night. "I did."

She cocked her head, her eyes on his. "And why would I go back with you?"

Why was she always so full of questions? "Because you love me."

Her head jerked up. "What?"

He knew he was in danger of losing her. He couldn't do it again, not after he'd taken her in his arms.

"All right, because I love you," he admitted. And then the dam just broke. Reason after reason flowed out. "Because Quint let me hit him because he knew that you had me tied up in knots inside. Because nothing at the ranch means anything now that you're gone." He leaned his forehead against hers. Hers was cool. His was throbbing. "Because I want you to come back and marry me. Satisfied?"

She encircled his neck with her arms, her grin spreading down to her toes. "Not yet, but I plan to be."

His lips were on hers before she could finish the last word. But even as he kissed her, a small, nagging doubt, raised by guilt, played across his mind.

When Kent drew back, Brianne looked at him, confused. He didn't look like a man who just had his proposal accepted. "What's the matter?"

"I can't ask you to give up your career."

Her grin was bathed in affection. There *was* a sensitive side to this man. It just took a long time to uncover. "Good, because I'm not going to."

It was his turn to look confused. "You're going to live here?"

Brianne laughed. The man was adorable. "No. I plan to live with you. But, through the miracle of computers, faxes, e-mail and teleconferences, I can still work on the magazine."

"So, you'll live with me." He repeated just to make it perfectly clear, and to assure himself that he wasn't dreaming.

Amusement danced in her eyes. "I'll live with you."

"Good, because it would have been a hell of a trek to your bedroom."

This time when he kissed her, there were no doubts, no guilt, nothing but desire ripening to passion.

Her editor, drawn by the vocal exchange, stuck his head in. Simon realized that his best photojournalist had brought back a souvenir. "Brianne, stop kissing that cowboy and finish that article for me."

She paused only long enough to look up. "In a minute," she promised.

By everyone's count at the magazine, it was the longest minute on record.

*   *   *   *   *

Look for Will's story in
WILL AND THE HEADSTRONG FEMALE,
coming to Silhouette Yours Truly
in November.

Books by Marie Ferrarella

Silhouette Yours Truly

†*The 7lb., 2oz. Valentine*
Let's Get Mommy Married
Traci on the Spot
Mommy and the Policeman Next Door
***Desperately Seeking Twin...*
The Offer She Couldn't Refuse
‡‡*Fiona and the Sexy Stranger*
‡‡*Cowboys Are for Loving*

Silhouette Romance

The Gift #588
Five-Alarm Affair #613
Heart to Heart #632
Mother for Hire #686
Borrowed Baby #730
Her Special Angel #744
The Undoing of Justin Starbuck #766
Man Trouble #815
The Taming of the Teen #839
Father Goose #869
Babies on His Mind #920
The Right Man #932
In Her Own Backyard #947
Her Man Friday #959
Aunt Connie's Wedding #984
‡*Caution: Baby Ahead* #1007
‡*Mother on the Wing* #1026
‡*Baby Times Two* #1037
Father in the Making #1078
The Women in Joe Sullivan's Life #1096
†*Do You Take This Child?* #1145
The Man Who Would Be Daddy #1175
Your Baby or Mine? #1216
***The Baby Came C.O.D.* #1264
Suddenly...Marriage!. #1312

Silhouette Special Edition

It Happened One Night #597
A Girl's Best Friend #652
Blessing in Disguise #675
Someone To Talk To #703
World's Greatest Dad #767
Family Matters #832
She Got Her Man #843
Baby in the Middle #892
Husband: Some Assembly Required #931
Brooding Angel #963
†*Baby's First Christmas* #997
Christmas Bride #1069
Wanted: Husband, Will Train #1132

Silhouette Desire

†*Husband: Optional* #988

Silhouette Intimate Moments

**Holding Out for a Hero* #496
**Heroes Great and Small* #501
**Christmas Every Day* #538
Callaghan's Way #561
**Caitlin's Guardian Angel* #661
†*Happy New Year—Baby!* #686
The Amnesiac Bride #787
Serena McKee's Back in Town #808
A Husband Waiting to Happen #842
Angus's Lost Lady #853

Fortune's Children

Forgotten Honeymoon

Silhouette Books

Silhouette Christmas Stories 1992
"The Night Santa Claus Returned"

‡*Baby's Choice*
†*The Baby of the Month Club*
*Those Sinclairs
***Two Halves of a Whole*
‡‡*The Cutlers of the Shady Lady Ranch*

Books by Marie Ferrarella writing as Marie Nicole

Silhouette Desire

Tried and True #112
Buyer Beware #142
Through Laughter and Tears #161
Grand Theft: Heart #182
A Woman of Integrity #197
Country Blue #224
Last Year's Hunk #274
Foxy Lady #315
Chocolate Dreams #346
No Laughing Matter #382

Silhouette Romance

Man Undercover #373
Please Stand By #394
Mine by Write #411
Getting Physical #440

Take 2 bestselling love stories FREE

Plus get a FREE surprise gift!

Special Limited-Time Offer

Mail to Silhouette Reader Service™

3010 Walden Avenue
P.O. Box 1867
Buffalo, N.Y. 14269-1867

YES! Please send me 2 free Silhouette Yours Truly™ novels and my free surprise gift. Then send me 4 brand-new novels every other month, which I will receive months before they appear in bookstores. Bill me at the low price of $2.90 each plus 25¢ delivery and applicable sales tax, if any.* That's the complete price, and a saving of over 10% off the cover prices—quite a bargain! I understand that accepting the books and gift places me under no obligation ever to buy any books. I can always return a shipment and cancel at any time. Even if I never buy another book from Silhouette, the 2 free books and the surprise gift are mine to keep forever.

201 SEN CH72

Name	(PLEASE PRINT)	
Address	Apt. No.	
City	State	Zip

This offer is limited to one order per household and not valid to present Silhouette Yours Truly™ subscribers. *Terms and prices are subject to change without notice. Sales tax applicable in N.Y.

MEN at WORK

All work and no play?
Not these men!

July 1998

MACKENZIE'S LADY by Dallas Schulze

Undercover agent Mackenzie Donahue's
lazy smile and deep blue eyes were his best
weapons. But after rescuing—and kissing!—
damsel in distress Holly Reynolds, how could
he betray her by spying on her brother?

August 1998

MISS LIZ'S PASSION by Sherryl Woods

Todd Lewis could put up a building with ease,
but quailed at the sight of a classroom! Still,
Liz Gentry, his son's teacher, was no battle-ax,
and soon Todd started planning some
extracurricular activities of his own....

September 1998

A CLASSIC ENCOUNTER by Emilie Richards

Doctor Chris Matthews was intelligent, sexy
and *very* good with his hands—which made
him all the more dangerous to single mom
Lizette St. Hilaire. So how long could she
resist Chris's special brand of TLC?

Available at your favorite retail outlet!

MEN AT WORK™

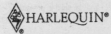 

Look us up on-line at: http://www.romance.net

PMAW2

Maternity Leave

Coming September 1998

Three delightful stories about the blessings
and surprises of "Labor" Day.

TABLOID BABY by Candace Camp

She was whisked to the hospital in the nick of time....

THE NINE-MONTH KNIGHT
by Cait London

A down-on-her-luck secretary is experiencing
odd little midnight cravings....

THE PATERNITY TEST by Sherryl Woods

The stick turned blue before her
biological clock struck twelve....

*These three special women are very pregnant...and very
single, although they won't be either for too much longer,
because baby—and Daddy—are on their way!*

Available at your favorite retail outlet.

**Available September 1998
from Silhouette Books...**

World's Most
Eligible Bachelors

THE CATCH
OF CONARD COUNTY
by Rachel Lee

Rancher Jeff Cumberland: long, lean, sexy as sin. He's eluded every marriage-minded female in the county. Until a mysterious woman breezes into town and brings her fierce passion to his bed. Will this steamy Conard County courtship take September's hottest bachelor off of the singles market?

Each month, Silhouette Books brings you an irresistible bachelor in these all-new, original stories. Find out how the sexiest, most sought-after men are finally caught...

Available at your favorite retail outlet.

Sneak Previews of October titles from Yours Truly™:

THE BAD-GIRL BRIDE
by Jennifer Drew

Nice girls finish last! So jilted Julie Myers was looking for
My-Fair-Lady lessons—in reverse! 'Cause to attract *more*
men, she figured she had to become a little *less* of a lady.
And she found the perfect instructor in rogue
Tom Brunswick. Trouble was, Tom's Habits for Highly
Effective Matchmaking were, uh, highly effective. And
while she could suddenly have her pick of handsome men,
she'd gone and fallen for the reigning expert on seduce-
and-resist—her teacher! While Tom was busy changing
Julie's good-girl image, had *she* somehow changed this
bad boy's mind about marriage?

THE ACCIDENTAL FIANCÉ
Women To Watch
by Krista Thoren

Gorgeous Grant Addison and strong-willed
Brianna Tully had to either pretend to be happily,
exclusively dating…or send their do-gooder sisters to
Matchmakers Anonymous! But that put-on gleam in
her eyes and that make-believe desire in his were too good
to be *false*…which fired up the family rumor mill and
sparked the colossal "accidental" announcement of
their impending wedding. Well, Brianna had no
intention of actually *marrying* her fiancé…even though he
secretly intended to make his mistaken bride-to-be
his real-life wife!